We've been shrunk!

Slowly, Russ climbed to his feet, dazed.

"Wh-what happened?" he asked, rubbing his head. "Where are we?"

They all looked at each other, the reality of the situation sinking in.

"We haven't gone anywhere," Nick said. "We're still *here*. We've been — shrunk, that's all."

HONEY, I SHRUNK THE KIDS

A Novel by Elizabeth Faucher
Based on the Motion Picture from Walt Disney Pictures
Produced by Penney Finkelman Cox
Based on the Screenplay by Ed Naha and Tom Schulman and
Story by Stuart Gordon & Brian Yuzna & Ed Naha
Directed by Joe Johnston

SCHOLASTIC INC.
New York Toronto London Auckland Sydney

ISBN 0-590-42115-8

12 11 10 9 8 7 6 5 4 3 2 1   9/8 0 1 2 3 4/9

Printed in the U.S.A.   01

First Scholastic printing, July 1989

Chapter 1

The neighborhood was a typical American suburb. Well-kept houses, neatly trimmed hedges, beautifully mowed lawns. The most typical house of all was the Thompsons' house — basketball hoop over the garage, station wagon in the driveway, ceramic animals around the yard in "lifelike" positions. Its owners undoubtedly won the Christmas lights contest year in and year out.

Russ Thompson walked out of the house, yawning. He was fifteen and small for his age — a fact that his father, "Big" Russ, never really let him forget. Russ's father had been a high school football star and constantly pushed his son to overexcel. Since Russ *liked* sports, he didn't really mind, but because of his size, he could never quite manage the achievements his father wanted.

But it was a nice morning, and if pumping iron made his father happy — hey, he'd pump some iron. He did a few stretching exercises, then jogged over to the garage, where his weight bench was. A birthday gift from his father when he was twelve.

Russ sat down on the weight bench, pushed his sweatshirt sleeves up, and took a deep breath. Then he picked up one of the smaller barbells to do some arm curls. Five sets of ten, to be exact.

Across the yard, his ten-year-old brother, Ron, was busy pitching a tent to spend the weekend in. *Noisily* pitching a tent. Ron was a gung-ho Lion Scout with a large imagination. To him, the yard, with its ceramic animals, was a jungle. Ron had a mischievous streak as deep as the Grand Canyon.

"Yo, Ron," Russ called over to him. "Keep it down, okay? You want to wake up Mom and Dad?"

"*You're* the one yelling," Ron called back, and kept hammering.

Russ shrugged and went back to his arm curls.

From the kitchen window of the house next door, Amy Szalinski watched the Thompson boys — Russ, in particular. If the Thompsons' house was the *most* conventional one in the neighborhood, the Szalinskis' was the least. At minimum, the house needed a coat of paint. Reshingling the róof, mowing the lawn, and weeding the garden wouldn't have hurt, either.

Amy, doing her best to cook breakfast for her father and brother, watched Russ working out until she smelled butter burning in the frying pan on the stove and had to dash to turn down the heat. Amy was also fifteen and pretty in spite of herself. She was taller than she wanted to be —

taller than Russ Thompson, for example — and self-conscious both about that and about wearing glasses. As a result, she had a tendency to slouch and duck her head whenever possible.

Her brother, Nicholas, who was nine, sat at the kitchen table, swinging his feet and reading a science fiction novel. He was very small for his age but several grades ahead academically. He also suffered from allergies, both real and imagined. When faced with a problem, he, more often than not, "played sick." To Amy's annoyance.

"Is breakfast ready?" he asked, reading.

"You're the one making the toast," Amy said, beating up six eggs with a fork, while taking out the pieces of shell that she had dropped in by accident. "Is the toast ready?"

"No," he said. "Are the eggs ready?"

"No," Amy said.

"Oh." Nicholas went back to reading.

"Did you put the toast *in* yet?" she asked, already knowing that he hadn't.

He lowered his book and looked at the toaster. "No. Not yet."

"Put the toast in," Amy said, patiently.

Nicholas put the toast in, then returned to his book.

Upstairs in the Thompsons' house, Mr. Thompson slowly opened his eyes after a loud clanging shattered the silence of the room where he and his wife were sleeping. Where they *had* been sleeping.

"What's that noise?" his wife, Mae, asked, her voice muffled by her pillow.

Mr. Thompson just groaned, swinging his feet over the edge of the bed to go see. He staggered over to the open window and gazed down into his backyard.

Ron was banging away on his tent stakes, making an incredible racket.

Mr. Thompson checked his watch, then stared down at his son. "What are you doing?" he asked gruffly.

Ron kept banging away merrily. "Pitching a tent, Dad," he said.

Mr. Thompson sighed. Deeply. "Don't you know that your mother and I are sleeping?"

"But," Ron pretended to be confused, "you're *talking* to me, Dad. I mean — well, you look awake."

His father growled something unintelligible, then looked over at the garage. "Having a good workout, son?" he called.

Russ, winded by bench presses, just waved.

"Perfect day for it," his father said, closing the window. He went back to bed, wincing as Ron continued hammering.

Mrs. Thompson smiled. "He's only a child."

"*Hitler* was a child once," Mr. Thompson said, and climbed underneath the covers.

"As long as you're up," Mrs. Thompson said, just as he got himself settled, "why don't you make us some coffee?"

Her husband stared at her. "What?"

She smiled brightly at him.

He sighed and got back out of bed, grabbing his battered New York Giants cap and tugging it down over his head.

"While you're up . . ." Mrs. Thompson said, terribly cheerful.

Mr. Thompson turned to look at her.

". . . how about some toast?" she asked.

He sighed, nodded, and went downstairs.

Over at the Szalinskis' house, Amy and Nicholas were still waiting for their toast.

"Is it ready yet?" she asked. "Are you watching it?"

He kept reading. "Yeah." He glanced at the frying pan, where the eggs were failing to scramble. "Mom never made them like *that*."

"Mom's not here," Amy said stiffly.

"Yeah." He paused. "Do you think she'll be home today?"

"I don't know," Amy said, reaching for a platter. "I hope so."

He stared at the gelatinous mess — vaguely resembling eggs — as she spooned it out of the pan, then sniffed it dubiously.

"I hope she comes back *soon*," he said.

Amy nodded, then saw smoke billowing out of the toaster, filling the kitchen. "Nick! The toast's on fire — you know what that means?"

"It's hot?" he guessed.

Amy sighed, unplugged the toaster, then extracted the blackened bread with a knife. "Straight-A student, and you can't make toast."

"I want to be a scientist like Dad," Nick said, "not a cook."

Amy looked around. "Where *is* Dad?"

Nick pointed with his fork. "Upstairs."

Amy sighed again. "Where else?"

Chapter 2

Upstairs in the attic, Wayne Szalinski — Amy and Nick's father — was putting the finishing touches on an electromagnetic pulse invention he had constructed. A good-natured, easy-going guy with a PhD in physics, he held a low-level job with an aerospace company and spent his weekends on his own work. Inventions, mostly. For Professor Szalinski, a bit of a scatterbrain in terms of day-to-day living, physics was easy. Wearing matched socks wasn't.

As he puttered around his worktable, the family's feisty little Yorkshire terrier, Quark, watched, mystified.

"This is it, Quark," Professor Szalinski said. "A red-letter day." He flicked a switch and the machine began to hum.

Quark backed toward the door.

"A common laser device, you say?" the professor asked as he adjusted a wire. Quark's ears flopped down in the canine version of a question mark. "Wrong, Quark. It's an amazing electromagnetic pulse device. If this baby works correctly, its computer scanners will hone in on a solid, inanimate object, analyze and isolate its molecular structure, and then reduce the space between its electrons. You know what that means, don't you?"

Quark cocked his head.

"It will actually *shrink* the object," Professor Szalinski said. "A boon to the space program. It will decrease the size and weight of payloads sent into space!"

Quark yawned and scratched behind his ear.

"Nifty, huh?" Professor Szalinski walked over to the couch and removed an apple from a small paper bag.

Quark perked up, barking and wagging his tail, in case it was snack time.

"Watch *this*," Professor Szalinski said, then walked over to a large steel plate the size of a wall and placed the apple on a pedestal in front of it. "The only real problem is that I haven't gotten the thing to work yet. But I'm close, Quark. Very, very close."

Finally realizing that the apple wasn't for him, Quark walked back toward the door, dejected.

Professor Szalinski put on protective goggles and activated the double-beamed machine. The two beams sparkled and came to life, buzzing harmlessly in the air. He adjusted the controls and they intersected, forming one solid shaft of light. The beam hit the apple, engulfing it. Light shimmered along the outside of the apple, which began vibrating wildly.

Quark cowered against the door.

"*Come on, shrink!*" the professor said, stepping back in anticipation. *"Shrink."*

There was a sudden blast and then the walls, Quark, and Professor Szalinski were covered with a small shower of — *applesauce.* Happily, Quark licked the sauce off his paws.

"Great." Professor Szalinski sighed and turned off the machine. He picked up his notes and a pencil, then flopped down on the couch to think. He sat upside down, his sauce-splattered head dangling over the edge of the couch. Quark's head loomed before him, upside down, and the dog began to lick the applesauce off his face.

"Bummer, Quark," Professor Szalinski said.

Quark wagged his tail, licking the applesauce.

"On the *plus* side," Professor Szalinski said, "we have discovered a very expensive way to make applesauçe."

Finished with his facial snack, Quark wagged his tail and trotted out of the room.

Professor Szalinski looked at his machine, then sat up and started making notes.

"Dad!" Amy yelled from downstairs. "Come and get it!"

Professor Szalinski tucked the pencil behind his right ear and walked out of the room. He paused in the hallway, then went back into the room, put the pencil down, picked up his papers, and left the room. He paused once more, went back in to get his pencil, then headed for the stairs.

He wandered downstairs and into the kitchen, diligently making notes, not watching where he was going.

"Dog," Amy said. It was something of a tradition for her to guide her ever-absentminded father into and out of rooms.

Without looking up, Professor Szalinski instinctively changed the direction of his left foot so as not to squash Quark.

"Nicholas," Amy said.

The professor pivoted, still reading his papers, making a move to sit down.

"Sewing kit," Amy said.

Professor Szalinski had almost landed on a small table housing a sewing basket. He lifted himself at the last minute and slid onto an adjoining chair.

After watching all of that, Nick sighed and began *his* morning routine, taking a series of pills from prescription bottles in front of him, each guaranteed to cure a different allergy.

Amy served the slimy eggs and half-raw bacon as her father continued to pore over his notes.

"Elbows up," she said.

Her father lifted his elbows and she slid his breakfast beneath them. He put down his notes and stared at the food.

"Umm." He put on a smile. "Looks *interesting*. What is it?"

"Scrambled eggs," Amy said, embarrassed.

Professor Szalinski touched the eggs with his fork. The slimy glop ran right through the prongs.

"Um, let me get you a spoon," Amy said quickly.

Her father nodded, reaching for a piece of toast. It was black. He tried to butter it, the toast crumbling on impact. He shrugged and went back to his notes, scribbling furiously.

Nick, very quietly, pushed his plate away. He poured a bowl of Cheerios and started eating them dry.

"What about your eggs?" Amy asked, hands on her hips.

"I'm allergic," he said.

She sighed, and turned to her father. "Did you pick up the refill on Nick's allergy pills, Dad?"

Professor Szalinski kept scribbling. "Mmmm."

"Dad," Amy said. "You promised. How could you forget? You were picking up my dress from the cleaners next door."

"Mmmm," he said, scribbling.

"You forgot the dress, too?"

Her father didn't answer, writing.

"Dad! I need that dress!" Amy said, exasperated. "There's a dance at school Friday night."

"It's not like anyone asked you to go," Nick said.

Amy scowled at him. "Well, someone *might*."

"Mmmm," their father said, obviously not paying attention.

"No wonder Mom left," Amy said. "All you think about is that stupid shrinking machine."

"It's not a shrinking machine," Nick said. "It's an *amazing* electromagnetic pulse device." Nick looked at his father, expecting a compliment; his father kept writing.

"It's a *dumb* machine," Amy muttered, then gestured toward her brother's bowl. "Put some milk on those."

Nick spooned up some dry Cheerios. "I'm allergic."

Amy took the cereal away and put the eggs back. "Then eat these."

Nick stirred the runny eggs with his fork. "Can I have a straw?"

Amy snatched the plate away. "Hey, if you don't want to eat it, fine. Quark will." She dumped the breakfast into the dog's bowl.

Quark got up, sniffed at it, then slunk away.

Nick laughed and took his cereal bowl back.

"Fine," Amy said, and gave up, pouring some cereal for herself.

Chapter 3

The Szalinskis were almost finished with breakfast when the phone rang.

"I'll get it," Amy said, starting to stand up.

"No, I'll get it!" Nick said.

"I've *got* it," their father said and hurried out to the phone in the hallway, still juggling his papers. He picked up the receiver, reading his notes. "Hello?"

"Wayne?" It was his wife, Diane. "It's Diane."

Professor Szalinski smiled, his notes momentarily forgotten. "Oh, hi, honey. Gee, I'm glad you called. We really missed you last night. How are you?"

Across town, at her mother's apartment, Diane smiled. She was very pretty, in her late thirties, with the same blonde hair Amy had.

"I'm fine," she said. She held back a sigh. "I just — called to remind you to take your suits to the dry cleaners."

"Oh, yeah," Professor Szalinski said. "Right."

"And," she added, "don't forget the food shopping has to be done today."

"Oh, right," Professor Szalinski said, having forgotten. "Thanks for reminding me."

Mrs. Szalinski couldn't help smiling. "You forget how long I've known you. How's the experiment going?"

"I'm close." Professor Szalinski brushed a stray splotch of splattered apple from his sleeve. Quark lapped it up from the floor. "Uh, really, really close."

"Well, I thought I'd wish you good luck today at the scientific conference," she said.

"Thanks. I'll need it." He shifted his weight to his other leg and the telephone to his other ear. "I mean, all I have are my theories, but, honey, if they go for them, they could fund my work for the next *year*. It'll be tough without physical proof, though." He frowned. "Scientists are weird."

"I never noticed," Mrs. Szalinski said wryly.

Flustered, Professor Szalinski shifted his weight. "Well — that is — "

"Well — " his wife hesitated. "You really miss me?"

"*A lot*," he said. "One hundred percent squared."

"That's funny. You never seemed to notice me when I was around."

He sighed. "I know, honey. I've just been so preoccupied with my work. I wish — why don't you come back home?"

Mrs. Szalinski didn't answer right away. "Maybe we can talk about it." Then she spoke more briskly. "Meanwhile, don't forget to pay the phone bill. And the gas bill and the electric bill are in the box in the cabinet. You'll need more detergent for the laundry. Fabric softener, too. And — Wayne, I miss you. I miss the kids. Do you think we can ever be a family again? A *real* family?"

Professor Szalinski didn't say anything — he was staring at his notes.

"Wayne?" his wife asked.

"Of course!" he said, very excited. "I know exactly what went wrong!"

"Really?" Mrs. Szalinski asked, catching the enthusiasm from him. "What?"

"It should have been x over y, not y over x," he said triumphantly. "The beams didn't meld — they collided!"

Mrs. Szalinski let out her breath, her enthusiasm gone. "You haven't heard a word I've said, have you?"

Guiltily, he lowered his notes. "I did. I said I missed you and you said" — he tried to think — "something back."

"You never change!" Mrs. Szalinski said, and slammed down the phone. Hard.

"Diane?" he asked. The dial tone blared in his ear. "Diane?" He put the phone down, seeing Amy in the doorway leading to the kitchen. "Uh, that was Mom. She says 'hi.' We — had a bad connection."

"Oh," Amy said, not convinced by his expression, but not about to argue, either. "I thought Nick and I would visit her today."

"No, no need," her father said. "She's coming over today."

"That's why she hung up?" Amy asked uncertainly. "Before talking to us, I mean?"

"What? I mean, yes," her father said. "That's why." He looked at his watch. "There's something I'm supposed to — ?"

"Meeting," Amy said.

Professor Szalinski nodded. "Right." With Amy and Nick trailing after him, he walked through the house, collecting his hat and coat and stuffing his papers into his battered leather briefcase. He stopped in his room long enough to put on a very loud tie, then headed for the front door, still holding a notepad in his hand, studying it as he walked. He reached for the doorknob and missed.

Amy opened the door for him. "Good luck, Dad."

"Hmmm," her father said vaguely.

"Good luck!" Nick chirped from the stairs.

After their father walked outside, Amy closed the door behind him. Amy and Nick looked at each other, mouthed the words "One, two, three," then looked at the door as it opened.

"Wish me luck, guys," their father said cheerfully.

Amy and Nick grinned at each other.

"Good luck, Dad," they said.

"I'll only be gone for a few hours." He closed the door and walked toward his car, seeing Big Russ and Mae Thompson in the garden separating the two houses.

Mrs. Thompson was tending to her pride and joy — her flower beds — tenderly removing barely visible weeds from around each plant. Her husband was watching her, his arms folded, full of not-very-helpful advice.

"Hey, Szalinski," he said gruffly, tipping up his New York Giants cap. "Working on a Saturday?"

"Yeah, Russ," Wayne said, extra-pleasant. "You know how it is."

Mr. Thompson didn't return the pleasant smile. "Thought maybe you'd fix up your yard today. Place looks like a *jungle*."

"Taken care of," Professor Szalinski said. "I hired the Pervis boy to cut the grass."

Mr. Thompson wasn't appeased. "Your *house* could use some sprucing up, too."

Mrs. Thompson frowned at her husband, distracted from her garden. *"Russell."*

Professor Szalinski just sighed — he and Mr. Thompson had had this exchange many times before. "Tell you what, Russ," he said. "If you'd like, I'll hire your construction company to fix it up. How's that?"

"No way." Mr. Thompson straightened his cap. "Olympian Construction doesn't diddle with small jobs. We only tackle the Big Stuff."

Professor Szalinski shrugged and got into his car. "Well, maybe someday I'll get a bigger house."

Mrs. Thompson chuckled as the professor pulled out of his driveway.

"Egghead," Mr. Thompson said. "I oughtta — "

Mrs. Thompson straightened up from the flower bed. "Forget about it."

"Yeah," Mr. Thompson said. "*That*, he wouldn't expect."

Mrs. Thompson smiled and turned her attention to the flowers on the side of the house, her trowel out and ready.

Seeing that she was occupied, her husband reached under his hat, pulling out a pack of cigarettes. He took one out, sniffed the tobacco, then placed it in his mouth, fumbling for a lighter.

"Russell?" Mrs. Thompson called, not looking up from her flowers. "You're not thinking of smoking, are you?"

He took the cigarette out of his mouth, stashing it and the pack back underneath his hat. "No, dear," he said sweetly. "You know I've given that up."

"You want to give me a hand with this mulch?" she asked.

"Certainly, dear," he said. "I can't think of anything nicer."

Chapter 4

Nick looked out the kitchen window, feeling lonely even with Quark sitting next to him. Amy, who spent most of her time doing housework these days, was downstairs in the laundry room; their father was at his meeting; their mother was away. He had been watching the Thompson boy put up his tent, wishing that even though he was younger, Ron would invite him to help.

But Ron didn't — probably didn't even *notice* him — so he sat in the window, constructing a small town out of Lego blocks.

Quark's ears went up and he began to growl, knocking over some of the Legos as he tried to climb onto the sill.

"What," Nick said, then spotted the Thompsons' cat, Cicero, out in the Thompsons' yard. Cicero was twice as big as Quark. "Forget it, pal," he said to Quark, and went back to the Legos.

Outside, Ron had finally gotten the tent up and was watching his brother, Russ, work out.

"Wanna have some *real* fun?" he asked.

"You're not going to try to dress up Cicero again, are you?" Russ asked.

The cat tensed.

"No, *better* than that," Ron said. Holding something behind his back, he stopped at the fence separating their yard from the Szalinskis' and produced a bottle of maple syrup. "Watch *this*."

Russ kept his distance. "Does Mom know you have that?"

Ron didn't answer, pouring a healthy wad of syrup on the fence. Flies began to land on it, getting trapped.

"Gotcha," he said cheerfully.

"What's so exciting about that?" Russ asked, not impressed.

"The *real* fun comes when we feed them to spiders."

Russ rolled his eyes.

Ron shrugged. "Hey, they're only *bugs*."

Escaping from the prospect of further garden work, their father came around the side of the house. He saw Ron, frowned, and walked toward him.

"Here comes Dad," Russ said. "He looks mad."

"Dad's always mad. Even when he's happy." Thinking fast, Ron threw the bottle over into the Szalinskis' yard, where the syrup emptied out into a patch of grass.

"What are you up to?" their father asked, frowning.

"Nothing, Dad." Ron gave him a big smile.

"I'm just watching bugs. Right, Russ?"

"Uh, yeah," Russ said.

"Oh." Mr. Thompson thought about that. "Well, don't watch the Szalinskis' bugs. Watch your *own* bugs."

"Yes, sir," Ron said. "Good idea, sir."

Their father nodded, heading for the weight bench to check on Russ's workout.

Seeing one of his baseballs lying under a bush, Ron picked it up. "Wanna play some ball?"

"I'm busy," Russ said.

Seeing his father, Russ did his bench presses with more energy.

"Better get a move on, son," his father said, checking his watch. "You're going to be late for football practice."

"Uh — " Russ sighed, lowering the weights. "Dad, I — "

"You've got to get out there early to get the edge on the other guys," his father said, clasping him on the shoulder and continuing past.

"Dad, I — " Russ sat up. "Dad?"

His father kept walking. "Come on, you don't want to be late."

"I-I'm not on the team anymore," Russ said. "I got cut."

"Because I know Coach Farrell always wants his players there on — " his father stopped. "*What?*"

Russ didn't look at him. "I got *cut*. I was too short and too light."

His father scowled. "Who said so?"

"Coach Farrell."

"Oh, he did, did he?" His father shoved his sleeves up, already looking for a fight. "Well, Bernie Farrell and I go back a long time — we played together. I used to knock him on his keister regularly." He clenched his fists. "Who does he think he is? I'll get him on the phone. Make him realize how important being on that team *is* to you!"

Russ sighed. "You don't have to, Dad. It's okay."

"It's *not* okay," his father said. "You're the son of *Big Russ Thompson*." He stormed toward the house, and the telephone.

Russ's mother, who had overheard this exchange from the garden, walked over to her son. "You told him?"

Russ nodded. "He didn't take it too well."

"Don't worry," his mother said. "I'll cool him down." Putting on a stern expression, she marched toward the back door.

Russ stared down at the weights, then sighed again, slumping onto the bench. Then he saw Amy out in her yard, tossing a Frisbee disc with Quark. He smiled at her, and she looked away. He sighed once more and returned to his bench presses.

Across the yard, Ron swatted the baseball high into the air, missing Russ by only inches as it came down. The ball bounced past Cicero, who yowled and leapt out of the way.

Russ didn't even have to look over to know where the ball had come from. "Knock it off, Ron," he said.

"What?" Ron asked, innocently.

"Hit it over here again, and you're going to be *dead meat.*" Russ forced the weights up again.

From his window, Nick watched Ron play.

"Better watch out!" he called. "You might hit that beehive." He pointed to a hive in a tree that straddled both yards.

Ron was not impressed. "What do you know about baseball, baby-brain? You can't play." He swung at the next pitch and connected. The ball missed the beehive by inches, rebounding off the tree and bouncing back down into the yard.

Nick gasped.

"Lucky guess," Ron said. But he changed the angle of his batting position, continuing his imaginary ballgame.

Not taking any chances, Nick pulled the screen down on his window, knocking a few Legos off the windowsill and into the yard. "Bees can kill you," he said. "If you're allergic. *I'm* allergic. I could die if I got stung."

"Oh, yeah?" Ron took a fast swing and sent the ball sailing over the fence separating the two yards until it smashed through the Szalinskis' attic window.

There was a long second of silence as Ron and Nick exchanged scared glances.

Hearing the glass shatter, Russ jumped up. "What did you do this time?" He looked at Ron.

"I didn't do it," Ron said.

Russ looked around until he located the broken glass. "Great. You busted the egghead's window."

Amy stormed over to the fence. "Can't you be careful?" she yelled. "Look what you've done! My dad is going to kill me when he comes home. And I'm going to tell him who did it, too."

"He's sorry," Russ said, and looked at his brother. *"Aren't* you?"

Up in the attic, the ball was perched precariously on a ledge directly above the electromagnetic pulse machine's inner workings. It teetered on the edge, then rolled off, smashing into the intricate, computer-chip-laden guts of the machine. It nestled in front of the power source of one of the two particle beam "cannons."

The machine sputtered to life. The computer went haywire, and the two gunlike laser devises began jerking back and forth, and up and down. However, only one of the laser beams was functioning, firing in short, crazy bursts.

ZZZAP! The beam hit Wayne's couch. There was a loud pop, and the couch shrank to miniature size. BZZAP! Pop! A chair went next. ZZZAP! Pop! Now, a trunk.

The machine was out of control.

Chapter 5

Out in the yard, Russ tried to calm Amy down.

"We'll get the window fixed," he promised. "We'll pay for it out of Ron's allowance."

"My allowance," Ron protested. "If anyone should pay for it, it should be baby-brain." He pointed at Nick, who had run out of the house to watch all of the excitement. "*He* made me move."

Amy put a protective arm around her brother. "I heard what Nick told you. You could have gotten stung by those bees and died if it wasn't for Nick."

Ron clasped his hands together. "My hero," he said, and batted his eyes.

"Actually," Nick said, "very few people die from bee stings. Unless you're allergic." He paused for effect. "I'm allergic."

Amy gave him a dirty look and removed her arm. "You're *not* allergic to bees," she said.

"I am, too!" he said. "I would've *died!*"

"Can't I at least have my ball back?" Ron asked, then knelt down in front of Amy. "*Puleeeze?*"

"Oh, all right." Amy moved aside. "Nick, take him upstairs and give him his stupid ball."

"Come on," Nick said, and led Ron into the house.

Amy and Russ were left standing in the yard. Aware that she was several inches taller, Amy tried — unobtrusively — to slouch.

Russ coughed. "I'm, uh, really sorry."

"You should be," Amy said huffily.

"Yeah." Russ tried to put his hands in his pockets, then remembered that he had on sweatpants. "I, uh, saw you throwing the Frisbee to the dog. You're pretty good."

Amy flushed a little. "Thank you."

"Yeah." There was no pocket on the front of his sweatshirt, so Russ just folded his arms. "You ever play with people? Frisbee, I mean?"

"Quark likes to fetch," Amy said, not really answering.

"Oh." Too shy to ask her if she wanted to play Frisbee with *him*, Russ bent down and picked up a small rock, flipping it away sidearm. "Well, Frisbees are a lot of fun."

"Yeah," Amy said. "I mean, Quark — I mean — "

"Yeah," Russ said, and they both blushed, looking in different directions.

Nick took Ron into the attic to retrieve the ball. Neither of them noticed that the machine had been activated, or that the computer screen was tracking their movements.

"Hey, check it out," Ron said, looking at the workbench. "It's right out of *Star Trek*."

"It's my dad's," Nick said proudly. "He works for an aerospace company."

"Thought he was a mad scientist," Ron said, hunting for the ball.

"No." Nick considered that in all seriousness. "He's pretty calm, actually."

As they searched, the working laser cannon began tracking Ron's movements. Neither boy noticed.

Seeing Nick facing the wall, frowning, Ron stopped hunting for the ball.

"What's wrong?" he asked.

"I don't know." Nick bit his lip, worried. "Something's *different*."

Ron stepped on something, which crunched underneath his foot. Curious, he bent down to see what it was.

"Hey, Nick," he said. "Look at all this neat stuff." He got down on all fours, staring at what had been the attic furniture — now one-quarter of an inch tall! "It looks like the prizes you get in Cracker Jack boxes, only better."

Behind him, there was a loud *pop* and a flash of light, and he turned.

"Hey, I know what it is," Nick said. "All my mother's furniture is gone!" He turned just in time to see the laser beams hit Ron, who instantly shrank! There was a loud zap and a huge flash of light — Nick was knocked to the floor.

He crawled over to where Ron had been standing, peering at the floor. Ron was there, as tiny as could be.

"Wow," Nick said. "It works!"

The machine began to aim its laser cannon

at him, and Nick realized what was about to happen.

"It works?" he said, feebly. He turned, just as the machine fired its beam at him.

Out in the yard, Amy and Russ were getting restless. Doggedly, he tried to keep their conversation going.

"Uh," he tried to think of a topic, "you like basketball?"

Amy bristled, straightening to her full height. "Why should I like basketball?"

Russ turned bright red. "Oh, I didn't — I mean, no reason. I just — lots of girls like basketball."

"Do you like *short* stories?" Amy asked, not appeased.

"Uh, well — " Russ blinked rapidly. "That is — "

A tall, gangly boy about their age came into the yard, eating from a bag of Oreos. It was Tommy Pervis, the boy Amy's father had hired to mow the lawn.

"Hey, Russ," he said with his mouth full. "Hi, Amy. Your dad around?"

Amy shook her head, still focusing on Russ.

"Oh. Well, if you see him, tell him I'll be a little late mowing the lawn. I gotta go shopping with my mom — she wants me to get new shoes." He indicated his jogging sneakers, which were splitting apart at the seams, then grinned at Russ. "Stupid, huh? These are just getting *good*."

"Mothers," Russ said, grinning back.

"Yeah." Tommy offered them the cookie bag,

and they both shook their heads. He helped himself to two more. "Catch you later," he said, ambling out of the yard.

"Yeah," Russ said. "Later, Pervis."

Alone again, Amy and Russ stood without speaking. Finally, Amy broke the silence.

"I'm going upstairs," she said. "That brother of yours better not be teasing Nick. You may not be able to control him, but *I* can." As she turned to go inside, she put her hand on the railing leading up the back steps, but pulled it back instantly. *"Aaahh!"*

"What is it?" Russ asked, ready to defend her. "What's the matter?"

"A *bug*." Amy shivered. "I hate bugs. It *touched* me."

Russ took his finger and flicked the bug off the railing to the ground, squashing it with his sneaker.

"Better?" he asked, making his voice a little deeper than usual.

"Hmmph," Amy said, not impressed. *"Murderer."* Then she walked — flounced, actually — into the house, leaving him behind.

Russ stood at the bottom of the steps, not sure what had just happened. Quark came over, wagging his tail, and Russ bent to pat him.

"You're lucky you're a dog," he said. Then, he took a deep breath and opened the door. "Amy? Wait up!"

He caught up to her just as she got to the attic door. "Hi," he said.

She smiled shyly. "What took you so long?"

Russ smiled back.

"Seems pretty quiet in there," Amy said, pushing the door open.

"Maybe they're hiding," Russ guessed. "Guys? Come on out."

Amy pushed the door open all the way, expecting them to jump out at her. "Nick?" she said cautiously. "Where are you?"

They stepped into the apparently empty room, not noticing that the machine had begun to track them.

Nick and Ron waved to get the big kids' attention.

"Russ!" Ron shouted, his voice squeaky. "Down here!"

"Amy!" Nick yelled, his voice even squeakier.

Not able to hear them, Russ and Amy moved across the attic in opposite directions.

"Nick?" Amy said. Slowly, she looked around the room, spotting the lights on her father's machine just as there was a ZZAP and she shrank.

She found herself on the vast floor of the attic, together with Nick and Ron. Found herself a quarter of an inch tall, stranded on a vast wooden plain. Shrunken furniture was everywhere.

Amy gazed around, stunned, then realized what had happened. She looked up at the titanic Russ, who was still roaming the attic. Then she spotted the now mammoth-looking machine, slowly aiming itself at him.

"Look out!" she yelled, as loudly as she could. Which wasn't very loud. At all.

In the normal-sized world, Russ glanced about for Amy, not sure how she could have vanished practically before his eyes.

"Amy?" he said, confused. "Where are you?" He turned all the way around, unaware of the machine focusing in on him.

"Look out!" Nick yelled.

"Go back!" Ron bellowed.

"Go get help!" Amy shouted. "Get my dad!"

Russ didn't hear the teeny-weenies, let alone see them. He glanced around the attic suspiciously, sure they were hiding somewhere. Hearing a strange buzzing sound, he turned around in time to see the laser cannon bobbing up and down, aiming in his direction.

As the staccato beams began firing at him, he jumped up and down, back and forth, ducking and dodging the bursts of light as well as he could, the machine-gunlike beams zipping all around him.

Every time his feet hit the attic floor, the teeny-weeny kids were tossed up and down into the air, the victims of a Russ-made earthquake. They tried to struggle to their feet and stay upright, but it was a losing battle. As Russ jumped closer to them, they scurried about, trying to stay out of the way of his shoes.

Ron flattened as the shoe came down on top of him. He was so small, however, that he fit between one of the grooves on the sole. The shoe lifted, leaving Ron unhurt as he rolled out of the way.

Russ continued his wild dance as the beams skittered by him. Finally, he ducked when he should have dodged and the beams connected. BZZAP! Pop! And he found himself on the floor, insect-sized. He lay there, groaning, completely in shock.

Meanwhile, the baseball, still balanced on the machinery, tumbled off the invention, unplugging it as it rolled. The ball bounced harmlessly onto the floor, past the four teeny-weenies.

There was a long, stunned silence.

"Hey," Ron said, finally. "Found the ball."

Amy, Nick, and Russ just looked at him.

"Terrific," Russ said.

"Thanks for telling us," Nick said.

"Any *more* news flashes?" Amy asked.

Chapter 6

Slowly, Russ climbed to his feet, dazed.

"Wh-what happened?" he asked, rubbing his head. "Where are we?"

They all looked at each other, the reality of the situation sinking in.

"We haven't gone anywhere," Nick said. "We're still *here*. We've been — shrunk, that's all."

"That's *all?*" Russ said.

"Why didn't you go for help?" Amy demanded. "All you had to do was — "

"How was I supposed to know what was happening up here?" Russ asked.

"You could have looked for us," Amy said.

Russ shrugged defensively. "I did."

"Well, then, you should have moved faster. Ducked the beams."

Since even now she was still taller than he was, Russ raised himself up on his toes to be her height. "Yeah," he said, "just like you did, right? If you're so smart, what do we do *now?*"

"Well — " Amy didn't say anything, stumped.

"I guess we just wait until my father gets home. He'll know what to do."

"He'll probably *step* on us," Russ said glumly.

Ron's eyes widened. "What?!"

"Don't worry," Nick said. "My father *always* knows what to do."

"Who's worried?" Ron asked, recovering himself. "I'm — *bored*."

"Yeah," Russ said, his voice more than a little ironic. " 'Boring' is the first word I thought of to describe this — " Now, *he* was stumped. "Situation," he said finally.

"Yeah," Amy said, looking around the seemingly endless expanse of wooden floor around them. " 'Boring' is the word I was looking for, too."

"*Really* boring," Nick said bravely.

"Totally," Ron said.

At the science convention, Wayne Szalinski's theories were greeted by the seriousness usually reserved for a stand-up comedy routine. He stood up in front of the group of scientists, scribbling equations on a blackboard with one hand, holding his papers in the other.

One young, arrogant scientist named Frederickson was being particularly hard on him. "What you're trying to say is that size is relative, uh, *Mister* Szalinski?" he said, his voice dripping sarcasm.

"Yes, I am," the inventor said, "*Professor* Frederickson."

"*Well*." Frederickson's smile was smug. "That's the most idiotic thing I've ever heard.

Size is definitive. What's big is big. What's small is small."

The crowd of scientists murmured assent.

"But you're wrong!" Professor Szalinski said. "My figures indicate that theoretically — "

"Where's your proof?" Frederickson wanted to know. "You have no *proof.*"

Professor Szalinski sighed, lowering his papers, aware that he was losing his audience. "When Einstein came up with theories that led to the atomic bomb, you didn't ask him to blow one up, did you?"

"You, Mr. Szalinski, are no Einstein," Frederickson said, and the crowd laughed. Sneering, Frederickson stood up and walked out of the room.

The rest of the scientists followed, leaving Professor Szalinski alone by the podium. An older, kinder scientist, Dr. Brainard, came over to him.

"Oh, hello, Dr. Brainard," Professor Szalinski said, gathering up his papers, trying to smile.

Dr. Brainard patted him on the shoulder. "Don't take it so hard, Wayne. Your ideas are very innovative. It will take time to convince people. I've had my share of problems with *committees,* too."

Professor Szalinski nodded, putting his notes in his briefcase. "They even laughed at my tie," he said sadly.

Dr. Brainard looked at the loud tie, holding back a smile with some difficulty. "Don't feel badly. *Anyone* would laugh at that tie."

Professor Szalinski grinned sheepishly.

* * *

When he got home, Professor Szalinski walked up to the house with his shoulders slumped. Quark ran out to greet him, barking.

"Hiya, Quark." The professor bent just enough to pat his head. "Okay. Treats. I know."

He walked into the kitchen and got Quark a Milkbone from the cupboard. Noticing the dirty breakfast dishes still in the sink, he frowned and turned toward the back door.

"Amy?" he called. "Nick? Where are you?"

Upstairs in the attic, the four kids perked up.

Nick was the first to scramble to his feet. "It's Dad!"

"Up here!" Amy yelled.

Russ cupped his hands around his mouth to try and amplify the sound. "Professor Szalinski!" he yelled. Ron shouted, "Yo! Hey, yo!" and banged on the floor with his tiny hands.

"He's never going to hear us," Nick said. "We're not loud enough."

"Just keep trying," Russ said, and they all yelled at once.

Downstairs, Professor Szalinski still didn't hear anything, so he walked out to the hallway.

"Kids?" he called. "I'm home. Amy? Nick?"

There was no answer and he shrugged, taking off his tie. He studied it briefly, frowned, and tossed it into the kitchen trash can. It landed among the remains of Amy's "sort of" scrambled eggs. Then he headed for the attic to work on his machine.

When he opened the door, the first thing he

saw was the broken glass from the window.

"Great," he said. "Just great!"

Amy and the others screamed and stamped their feet, trying to get his attention.

"Dad! We're down here!" Amy clapped her hands, too, making as much noise as she could.

Russ joined in. "Professor Szalinski! Over here!"

"Egghead!" Ron contributed.

Russ punched him, hard, on the arm.

"Uh, Professor Szalinski!" Ron said, more politely.

Above them, Wayne saw that glass fragments were scattered on top of his machine. Which didn't exactly make his day.

"What *else* can go wrong," he grumbled, backed over to where his old, reliable couch had once stood, and sat down.

There was no couch. When he crashed down to the floor, the force of the impact sent the teeny-weenies tumbling.

"Oh, great. Who would break into an attic and steal an old couch?" Professor Szalinski got up, brushing himself off. "That's it. That does it — I've had it. I've had it with everything!" He strode out of the room, while Amy and the others shouted squeakily in protest.

"Dad! Come *back!*" Amy said.

Nick sat down unhappily. "He can't hear you."

Russ sat down, too. "I thought he was going to *save* us, remember?"

"He was upset," Amy said. "That's all."

Russ kicked at a floor splinter that looked as big as a baseball bat. "He's not the *only* one."

"Well, he had every right to be. This — " she gestured dismissively at Ron — "*twerp* smashed Dad's machine with his stupid baseball."

"Who you calling a twerp, beanpole?" Ron asked. "Huh?"

The four kids felt the floor beneath them begin to shudder, footsteps rumbling ominously in the background.

Nick jumped up, excited again. "It's Dad — he's coming back!"

The door opened and a shadow fell over them all.

"Oh, *no*," Amy said.

"What?" Russ asked, hearing the fear in her voice.

"He's going to *clean up*," she said.

Indeed, the professor had come back with the kitchen trash can, a broom, and a dustpan.

"What do we *do?*" Nick asked, coughing from the dust that was raised as his father began sweeping up the broken glass.

"Scatter!" Russ said.

They tried to run, but it was no use. They were caught up by the broom and swept into the dustpan. Wayne carried the dustpan over to the open trash can as the five of them jumped up and down, trying to get his attention.

"Dad, please!" Amy waved both arms through the dust surrounding her.

"Don't!" Nick yelled, coughing from the stray bits of dog fur that had gotten swept up, too. He was allergic to dog fur.

"Professor Szalinski!" Russ picked up a piece

of white paper, trying to signal him with it. "It's us!"

"Just knock it off!" Ron ordered. "You hear me?"

Neither hearing nor seeing them, Mr. Szalinski tipped the dustpan up, and they went tumbling through space, down into the trash. They landed on top of one another, tangled together, slipping and sliding among the various wads of junk before coming to a stop.

Then it got very, very dark.

"Wh-what's happening?" Ron asked, his voice shaking.

Amy saw the top of the bag twisting closed. "I think he's going to throw us away," she said.

Chapter 7

Professor Szalinski fastened the top of the garbage bag with a small green wire, then hefted it up onto his shoulder and carried it downstairs. Quark ran along behind him, whining madly and sniffing at the bag.

The professor nudged him back inside the house with one foot as the dog tried to follow him out to the backyard.

"Quark," he said sternly. "This *isn't* for you. It's garbage. You've had your treats." He closed the door in Quark's face, carrying the bag outside. He put the bag down near the rear fence, next to several other garbage bags, then returned to the house.

Quark met him at the door, barking and whimpering. Professor Szalinski ignored him, sitting down at the kitchen table.

"Not now," he said, resting his head in his hands, "okay, Quark?"

Quark slunk off into his corner, lying pensively in his dog bed, glancing at the door leading to the backyard. He whined once more, got a stern look from Professor Szalinski, and subsided.

Inside the trash bag, no one said anything for a minute. They were all jumbled together in near-total darkness.

"*Yecchh*," Ron said finally. He sniffed the rather putrid air. "What is this junk? More of your father's experiments?"

"They're *eggs*," Amy said, and Nick laughed. She tried to find him in the bag, to hit him, but hit Russ instead.

"Ow," Russ said, and assuming that it had been Ron, tried to hit *him*, hitting Nick instead.

"Ow! Cut it out, Ron!" Nick hit Amy, who yelped.

"Sure is dark in here," Ron said.

"Unless we get out of here," Nick said quietly, "we're going to be taken to the dump in two days."

It was silent.

"Lion scout Thompson to the rescue!" Ron grabbed the camping knife he still had in his pocket, jabbing it into the side of the bag.

Outside, they saw a strange, giant world.

"Come on, let's get out of here," Amy said, trying to move past the awe-struck Ron.

"Quit shoving," Ron said.

"I'm not," Amy said, and pushed him so she could get by.

They climbed out of the bag. Russ gave Nick a helping hand down to the ground.

"There!" Ron said proudly, sliding his knife back into his pocket. "Nothing to it."

"Check it out," Nick said, staring at the world around them.

They all looked around, amazed by what they were seeing. From their quarter-inch height, the backyard was a totally alien landscape: large, green, never-ending . . . and *dangerous*.

Before them lay a redwood-forest-sized sea of grass, shadow-laden and foreboding, with only a stray ray or two of sunlight illuminating the ground. They stared somberly into the dark jungle.

"Kind of brings a new dimension to the word 'grounded,' " Ron said.

No one laughed.

"Okay, okay," Amy said, thinking aloud. "Our only hope is to get back to the house. If Dad's machine can *shrink* us, it can enlarge us, too. Right, Nick?"

Nick was looking at the never-ending terrain stretching out before them, his mouth hanging open.

"Nick?" Amy said again.

"I, uh — I guess he could reverse the process," Nick said softly.

"Good." Amy nodded to punctuate that. "Then all we have to do is get across the yard."

Nick started sneezing and pulled some Kleenex out of his pocket.

Russ nudged Amy. "What's with him?"

Amy sighed. "He's allergic."

"Oh." Russ watched him as he continued to wheeze. "To what?"

"Life," Ron laughed.

Amy scowled at him, then turned to Russ.

"Look. Maybe you and your brother had better go back to the house on your own. I don't know if Nick can make it."

Russ shook his head. "That doesn't sound very — "

"The beanpole's right," Ron interrupted. "The wimpoid'll just slow us down."

Amy put her hands on her hips. "Do I look like I was talking to *you?*"

"No," Ron said. Politely.

"Right." Amy turned back to Russ. "If you go, you can come find us later."

"Don't worry about *me*," Nick said. "I can make it."

"You know how you get when you're outside too long," Amy reminded him. "You can't breathe."

Nick put his Kleenex away, looking stubborn. "I can do it."

"We'll go together," Russ said. "Period. Got it?"

The others nodded.

"Good." He gazed into the forest ahead of them. "So, the plan is to get back to the house, right?"

The others nodded.

"Then let's do it," he said, and started forward.

"Which way?" Amy asked, hanging back.

Russ hestiated. "Straight ahead. I guess."

"Okay." Amy walked behind him, motioning for the others to follow.

They walked deep into the underbrush, Nick sneezing every so often. There was very little light, since the sky was blocked by the waving greens above them. There were noises all around them — buzzing, crackling, chomping. *Scary* noises.

Suddenly, Ron let out a Tarzan yell, stopping everybody else dead in their tracks.

"What?" Nick asked, looking around wildly. "What is it?"

Ron shrugged. "Hey, this is supposed to be an adventure, right?"

Russ turned, showing him his fist. "Knock it off."

"Hey, don't pick on *me*, pal," Ron said. "You're not even sure we're going the right way."

Russ looked at Amy. "He has a point."

Amy gestured at the impenetrable vegetation. "Got any bright ideas?"

Russ thought for a minute, then climbed a blade of grass as if it were a tree, gazing into the distance. There, looming like Mount Everest, surrounded by the swirling expanse of grass, was the Szalinskis' house — seemingly a hundred miles away.

The other four clustered around the base of the blade of grass, peering up.

"Can you see the house?" Amy asked.

"Sure can." Russ slid down the grass to the dirt below, landing with a thump. "We can probably get there by sundown. Follow me."

"Wait a minute," Amy said, not trusting the overconfidence in his voice. "You don't know your way around this yard. You could walk us into a ditch."

Russ smiled patiently at her. "I'm the oldest, okay?"

"You are not," Amy said. "Besides, *I'm* the biggest."

Russ stepped up to her, flexing his biceps. "You're just a *girl*."

Nick cleared his throat, breaking the standoff. "You're *both* the oldest. Why don't you *both* take charge?"

Amy and Russ eyed each other cautiously.

"Sounds good," Russ said.

"All right," Amy said.

They walked forward, the other two falling in behind them.

"I don't believe it," Ron said aloud. "Russ siding with some *girl*."

"Just walk," Russ said, already tired.

Amy and Russ forged ahead, doing their best to blaze a path through the impossibly thick grass.

"You forget just how big this world can be sometimes," Amy said, gazing around.

Russ shrugged. "When you're short, you think about it *a lot*."

Amy let that pass. "Do you really think we can make it back to the house today?"

Russ checked behind them to make sure that the others were too far away to hear. "I don't know," he said. "It looked pretty far. I didn't want to scare the kids though."

Amy nodded, shivering slightly.

"Look," Russ said. "I know we're not — friends — or anything, but — "

"We're not?" Amy said.

"Well — " Russ stopped. "I don't know. Don't we just mostly fight?"

"Well, yeah, but — " Amy blushed. "I thought we were *kind of* friends."

"Oh." Russ thought about that. "I mean, you think so?"

"I *thought* so," Amy said.

"Oh. Okay. I mean, I thought that — I mean, it seemed like — " He stopped again, also blushing. "I don't know what I thought."

"Well, what were you going to say?"

"I just — " He glanced over his shoulder at the two boys struggling toward them, their progress slow. "We should act like we know what we're doing. If the little kids get discouraged, they'll punk out on us."

"Okay," Amy said. "Then we will."

"Okay," Russ said, and they exchanged shy smiles.

"How far have we gone?" Nick asked, out of breath.

"Pretty far," Amy lied. "You're doing great."

Suddenly, a titanic shadow passed overhead; all of them froze.

"Whew," Ron said, relaxing as a huge butterfly flapped harmlessly by.

As they pushed on, Ron heard a strange sound. He cocked his head, motioning for the others to listen, too. They stopped as the sound of prolonged thunder ripped through the forest.

"Hey, what's that?" Nick pointed up ahead. The grass was blowing in all directions, twigs and blades flying up into the air.

"Pretty weird," Ron said.

"Look at *that*," Nick said, as a tremendous dandelion launched itself into space. The two boys exchanged wondering looks.

The approaching storm built in fury. Blasts of wind howled through the blades of grass, ruffling their hair and clothes. The group stopped walking.

"We'd better get moving," Russ said uneasily.

The earth began to shake violently beneath them, knocking them this way and that. They managed to get back to their feet by clinging to the tree-sized roots of the grass and weeds, the whole world in turmoil around them as squalls of dusty wind surrounded them.

"It's got to be an earthquake," Russ said, trying not to panic.

Nick squinted into the grit, wheezing. "Worse," he said. "It's a lawn mower."

Chapter 8

The four of them gaped at the approaching maelstrom. The Oreo-munching Tommy Pervis, now the size of the Jolly Green Giant, was pushing a King-Kong-sized power mower. The gas-powered machine was shredding grass and tossing the debris into the bag attached to its rear. Some of the debris, however, missed the bag and came crashing down onto the forest floor like an avalanche of uprooted trees.

Knocked down by the tornado-like winds, the four scrambled to their feet, trying to outrun the machine, while large, boulder-sized pieces of grass smashed down onto the ground all around them.

"Get down!" Russ yelled. "Get down and maybe it'll go over us!"

They all flung themselves to the ground, clinging to grass roots for dear life as the machine rumbled toward them. Everywhere, the grass was being obliterated, sucked into the engine, then blasted helter-skelter across the floor of the yard.

"Hold on tight!" Russ yelled.

The bottom of the mower hovered above them like an ominous mother ship from some alien planet. Its blades whirled madly. They clung to each other as their feet began lifting from the ground. They were being drawn to the mower by the whirling suction.

"Grab hands!" Russ yelled, trying to hold all of them down. "Grab hands!"

They formed a human wheel, like skydivers in formation, anchoring each other as the mower passed directly over them. Ron, hanging onto one of Amy's hands and one of Russ's, let out a brief, terrified shriek as the suction lifted his legs into the air. He lost his grip and was torn from the others.

"Ron!" Russ stared, horrified, as his brother swirled high above them, then was sucked into the churning blades.

Ron hung on frantically to a tree-trunk-sized grass stem, his feet still being pulled upward, and then he disappeared. The machine whirled above the other three for another long moment, its noise deafening.

A large, brand-new sneaker smashed down onto the ground near them, then rose, only to smash down just ahead of them. They were buffeted about for a few more seconds, then gradually the noise subsided, the mower moved on, the thunder faded away.

They climbed out from underneath a blanket of shredded grass, green slabs about the size of surfboards.

"Ron!" Russ called, anxiously, "Ron!"

"He's in here somewhere," Nick said. "He *has* to be."

They searched frantically, calling out his name.

"Ronald!" Amy shouted, throwing grass aside as quickly as she could. "Ronald, where are you?"

"Come on, don't kid around," Russ said, his voice shaking. "Come on out."

They searched for several tense minutes, then stopped to catch their breath, too horrified to look at one another.

"Hey!" Ron bellowed. "I'm over here!"

They turned and saw Ron, a city block away, hanging precariously from the tip of a shredded dandelion stalk. They all gasped as he lost his grip and fell out of view. But, almost instantly, he reappeared, flying up in the air. They ran toward him as he bounced up and down.

As they got closer, they saw a giant forest of flowers; it was just a few feet of an overgrown wildflower bed in the Szalinskis' yard. Ron was bouncing up and down on a flower, using it as a trampoline.

"Hey, this is fun!" he said. "Come on!"

Amy and Russ stood there, watching him bounce.

"It's *beautiful*," Amy said, staring at what looked like flower paradise.

"Yeah." Russ coughed, embarrassed by the awe in his own tone. "I mean — it's okay."

"It looks like *Oz*," Nick breathed.

Ron, discovering that the shorter flowers were even better trampolines, bounced up and down from one flower to another.

"Up, up, and away!" Ron yelled, bouncing into the air.

"Be careful — you might hurt yourself." Russ shook his head. "I can't believe I just said that." He looked at Amy, who had fashioned a hula skirt around her belt with large flower petals.

"Oh, honey," she said. "I just *have* to have this dress."

Russ grinned. "Cut it out, will ya?"

"Please, dear?" Amy clasped her hands together. "We can charge it."

Nick giggled.

Ron bounced past a dandelion puff, which disintegrated, and rained down a shower of flowery "snow." This made the flower bed look even more like a fairyland. Nick began rolling around in the "snow," sneezing.

"Are you okay?" Amy asked, worried.

"It's *just* hay fever," Nick said. "I'm fine." He puffed out his chest, running into the maze of flowers.

Ron was shouting at the top of his lungs, bouncing from flower to flower. Hesitantly, Nick tried a bounce on a small flower, landing awkwardly. He tried another, and then another, winding up on the ground. Hearing Amy and Russ laugh, he was going to quit, but realizing that the laughter wasn't malicious, he picked himself up. He climbed back onto the flower and began bouncing, gradually getting the hang of it.

"Yahoo," he whispered and then, gaining courage, yelled as loudly as he could. "Yahoo!"

Russ and Amy smiled, watching their brothers play.

"So," Amy said. "You check out Tommy's new sneakers?"

Russ laughed. "Are you serious?"

"Oh, yeah," Amy said. "You should get a pair like them."

"Uh-huh." Still smiling, he looked up at the sky, at the sun. "We'd better get moving." He raised his voice. "Come on, guys! We've got a lot of ground to cover before it gets dark."

Nick stopped bouncing immediately; Ron pretended he didn't hear.

"Come on, Ron," Russ said, more firmly.

Ron shook his head, bouncing in the air. "No way, José."

"I'm not kidding," Russ said. "I'm counting to five."

"You're beginning to sound a lot like Dad," Ron said. "Scary, huh?"

Russ wasn't amused. "Ronald."

"Come on," Ron said to Nick, who was obviously torn between fun and obedience. "What are you stopping for? We're having fun, right?"

Nick nodded. "But Russ said — "

" 'But Russ said,' " Ron mimicked his voice. "What a wuss."

Russ strode forward, yanking Ron from his flower.

"Hey!" Ron tried to get away. "Cut it out, you wanna hurt me or something? I'll tell Mom!"

Russ lifted him off the ground, holding him still so he could look into his eyes. "There's something you'd better understand," he said quietly. "We're in a lot of trouble, okay? This isn't a game. We could die out here and no one would notice.

The only way we're going to get out of this is if we all help each other. Got that?"

Ron nodded solemnly. "Uh-huh."

Russ put him down. "Good."

Ron immediately ran back to a flower and launched himself up onto a flower-trampoline. "But first," he said, "playtime!" Ron started bouncing again.

Nick laughed and resumed the game as well, Amy and Russ exchanging exasperated glances.

"Can't you control him?" Amy asked.

"Hey, *your* brother's fooling around, too," Russ pointed out.

"I know, but — " Amy paused, hearing a faint buzzing. "What's that?"

Russ listened, his head tilted toward the sky. "It sounds like a buzz saw. It's probably my father."

Amy shook her head. "It's coming from different directions."

"No way," Russ said. "It's just your ears playing tricks on you."

"Will you shut up and listen?" Amy asked impatiently.

Russ glowered but closed his mouth.

The buzzing, indeed, seemed to be coming from all around them. Up on the flowers, the others stopped bouncing, listening to the buzzing, which grew louder and louder, sounding like the streets of London during the Nazi Blitz.

Then Amy screamed, pointing at a dark cloud above them. It was an enormous honeybee swooping down over the flowerbed.

"Hit the dirt!" Russ yelled.

Ron dove off his flower and ran in one direction, Nick scurried off in another; Amy and Russ dropped in their tracks.

The honeybee hovered over the flowers, then landed on one, extracting the pollen and stuffing the sticky yellow stuff into natural pouches on its rear legs. It moved from flower to flower, looking as big as a flying Volkswagen van.

Nick crouched below a yellow flower, wheezing. The bee alighted right next to him, descending lower and lower. Nick trembled, trying to make himself smaller. Invisible.

"Shhh," Russ said, putting his hand over Amy's mouth as she started to yell.

Nick watched, mesmerized, as the bee flew closer and closer. Suddenly, the bee scooped him up, plastering him onto one of its hind legs, along with the sticky pollen.

Amy broke away from Russ, running toward the bee. "Nick!"

"Holy cow!" Ron gasped.

"Amy!" Nick wheezed, half smothered in pollen.

Russ sprang forward and leapt onto a flower, using it as a trampoline. "I'll get him!" He bounced from flower to flower, sailing through the air toward the bee. As it took off, satiated, Russ dove onto its back, hanging onto a piece of pollen.

Amy and Ron watched, fearfully, as the bee, along with Nick and Russ, disappeared into the sky.

Chapter 9

The two of them stared, transfixed, as the humming noise faded away.

"Oh, no." Amy ran blindly into the grass forest, in the direction the bee had flown. "Nick! Russ!"

"Wait for me!" Ron yelled as he chased after her.

Meanwhile, on the back of the bee, Russ was getting a breathtaking — and dizzying — ride high above the yard. The bee twisted and turned, as Russ fought to get control of it by grabbing its wings, trying not to fall off its back. Below him, Nick squirmed around in the sticky pollen.

"Russ, help!" he said weakly. "Help me!"

"Hold on tight, Nick!" Russ shouted down to him. "Just hang on!"

The bee careened over the yard, annoyed by the weight of its surprise baggage. Far below them, Tommy Pervis was standing near the house, surveying the newly cut grass. Struggling for control of the bee's wings, Russ saw that they were heading straight for Tommy's head.

"Tommy!" he shouted. "Look out!"

Hearing a sort of squeaking, and then a buzzing, Tommy looked up. Confused, he started swatting at the bee.

"G'wan." He waved it away. "Get outta here."

Ducking Tommy's swings, the bee veered away, heading for its beehive. Realizing that that would be the end for them, Russ grabbed one of the wings, giving it a solid yank. Unable to control its flight, the bee began a spiraling dive toward the ground. Russ and Nick both yelled as they hurtled straight down.

The bee landed nose first in the dirt with a sickening crash, sending both boys tumbling off. The insect and the two boys lay inert on the ground.

Amy and Ron wandered deeper into the jungle.

"We're never going to find them," Amy said.

"We'll find them," Ron said confidently. "I'm a scout."

Amy shook her head, lost in the endless sea of grass. "I think we should go back to the flower bed and wait. We promised Russ — "

"*You* promised," Ron said. "I say we should go after them. You're just chicken."

Amy scowled at him. "If I were your sister, I'd spank you until you couldn't sit down."

"If you were my sister, I'd put myself up for adoption. I'm going to find Russ and the wuss. You coming or what?" He stalked off into the forest.

Amy hesitated, watching Ron disappear. Then she gritted her teeth and went after him.

Up in the house, Wayne Szalinski was on the phone, trying to call his wife, Diane. Getting the answering machine. He slammed the phone down.

Quark sat at his feet, whining.

"I know, I know," he said. "Lunchtime." The doorbell rang and he walked to the front door. "It's not like Amy and Nick to miss lunch without letting me know."

He yanked the door open and saw his wife standing there. They stared at each other.

He poked his head outside and looked to the left and the right, expecting to see Amy and Nick. Except that they weren't there. Puzzled, he stepped back inside the house, motioning for her to enter, and closed the door behind them.

"Where are the kids?" he asked.

"*What?*" she said.

"I thought they might be with you."

"They probably went to the mall," she said.

"Yeah," Professor Szalinski replied. "Kind of strange though. Somebody broke into the attic and stole my couch."

"Out of the attic?" Mrs. Szalinski asked. She suddenly grew concerned. "Wayne, where are the kids?" She walked into the kitchen, looking for them.

Professor Szalinski trailed after her, Quark whining next to him. "I haven't seen them since this morning."

"Quiet, Quark," she said, looking out the window into the empty backyard.

Quark barked.

"Quiet, Quark," he said, and put a thoughtful finger to his lips. "Hmmm. I *did* forget to pick up Amy's dress and Nick's pills."

Mrs. Szalinski sat down at the kitchen table, shaking her head. "Oh, Wayne."

"Well, you didn't remind me," he said defensively.

Quark barked.

"Quiet, Quark!" they both said.

Quark barked, scratching on the back door.

They looked at each other and walked outside, leaving Quark in the house.

Wayne Szalinski stood on the back steps, his wife behind him. "Amy? Nick? Are you out here?"

Deep in the forest, Amy and Ron heard a thundering roar, so loud that they could barely make out the words.

The roar came again. "Amy? Nick!"

Amy ran forward. "It's my father — come on!" She and Ron ran in the direction of the roar, yelling and waving their arms.

Meanwhile, Mr. Thompson walked out into his backyard, where his wife had progressed from weeding to *watering* her garden.

"Ron!" he called. "Russell!"

Ron skidded to a stop, hearing him.

"It's Dad!" Ron said eagerly.

He started running in that direction instead. "Dad! Over here!"

Mr. Thompson, spotting Professor Szalinski, walked over to the fence. He leaned his arms on it, coming up with an elbowful of maple syrup. He frowned as Professor Szalinski came toward him.

"Yard looks a little better, Szalinski," he said. "You should get a nice flower garden going over there."

"Begonias would be nice," Mrs. Thompson said, spraying her flowers.

"I've always meant to . . ." Mrs. Szalinksi's voice faded off. "There's never time. . . ."

Professor Szalinski changed the subject. "Hey, have you seen my kids?"

"No," Mr. Thompson said. "I was just looking for mine. They *never* miss lunch."

"Mine, either," the professor said.

Mr. Thompson's eyebrows came together. "Can't figure it out. On Saturdays, they're always hanging around. Always underfoot."

As the voices changed directions, Amy and Ron did, too, running as fast as they could.

"Mom! Dad!" Amy shouted, her voice getting hoarse.

"Come on, Dad!" Ron yelled, frustrated. "We're over here!"

They ran breathlessly forward, shouting to their parents.

"It's no use," Amy panted. "They can't hear us."

"I thought your father was a genius," Ron said, gasping for breath.

"He still has normal *ears*," Amy said.

They ran harder. Faster.

The parents stood on either side of the fence. Mrs. Thompson held the garden hose.

"It's nice to see you, Diane," she said, smiling.

Mrs. Szalinski nodded her head. "You wouldn't happen to have seen Amy or Nick, would you?"

"Sorry. We've misplaced *ours*, too." Mrs. Thompson said. "I'm sure they'll turn up for supper."

Mrs. Szalinski nodded. "You're probably right. Good to see you, Mae."

As the Szalinskis walked back to their house, Mrs. Thompson finished watering her lawn. She turned off the nozzle of the hose, then glanced at the Szalinskis' backyard, where the grass was dry and beginning to yellow.

She clicked her tongue. "Tsk-tsk. Poor grass." She turned the nozzle back on, sending a steady stream of water over the fence and into the yard.

Amy and Ron staggered along through the forest, even though they couldn't hear their parents' voices anymore. Suddenly, they were surrounded by huge, falling raindrops splashing all around them.

"*Now* what," Amy said, already drenched.

"Flood!" Ron said, and dove into a nearby hole for shelter. Amy crawled in after him.

They screamed and ran out as a large pink worm slithered after them, chasing them out of the hole. Still screaming, they ran for their lives.

Humming merrily, Mrs. Thompson kept spraying the yard. Deep pools of water formed. *Very* deep for anyone who was only a quarter of an inch tall.

Chapter 10

Russ and Nick slowly sat up, dizzy and weak. As they did, they saw the bee shake itself awake as well. It was *very* angry and, spotting the two of them, began to advance, its wings buzzing ominously.

"Are you strong enough to run?" Russ said, helping Nick to his feet.

"Y-you bet," Nick said.

They tried to run, but the bee darted toward them. It was almost on top of them. Suddenly it was knocked out of the air by a gigantic droplet of water. The two boys stopped, puzzled.

"Are we safe?" Nick asked.

"I'm not sure," Russ said uneasily.

Then, enormous droplets of water began falling around them. Within seconds, the ground beneath their feet turned to mush, as the yard slowly filled up with water.

"Come on, up here!" Russ climbed up a blade of grass, pulling Nick up behind him.

They hung on tightly, their weight swinging the blade of grass back and forth.

* * *

Humming and humming, Mrs. Thompson watered away.

Amy and Ron ran from a wall of water that rose behind them, knocking over stalks of grass in its path.

"Head for higher ground!" Amy yelled, stumbling through the muddied dirt.

They ran, but the tidal wave of water came closer and closer.

"What do we do?" Ron asked, his voice high with terror.

Amy looked around frantically. "I don't — there!"

Ahead of them, a giant bottle cap lay in the dirt. Amy ran to it, grabbing Ron and hurling him inside by his belt just as the water caught up with them. She tried to climb on board but couldn't quite make it, clutching the metal rim as the flood carried the cap away.

Pulling and tugging, Ron helped Amy drag herself inside. Before they knew what was happening, they were taken for a spiraling white water rapids ride, the bottle cap spinning around as the water rushed through the yard.

Amy and Ron gripped the sides of their boat as it bumped and zigzagged through the raging river, like a waterborne Tilt-a-Whirl car, completely out of control.

Russ and Nick hung onto their grass blade, the water rushing below them. The torrent's force uprooted the entire blade and they zipped down the current on a grass "canoe." The grass blade dipped up, then plunged down over a small waterfall, the two boys yelling in protest. Or fear.

In the meantime, the bottle cap had begun to take on water. Amy and Ron used their hands to try and bail the water out of the spinning cap, but the flood sloshed in faster than they could bail.

The bottle cap careened down the river toward Russ and Nick and their grass canoe.

"Russell! Nick!" Amy waved her arms. "Help, we're sinking!"

Russ and Nick used their hands as paddles, trying to bring the grass blade alongside the cap. The two storm-tossed crafts zigzagged closer and then further away from one another. Amy and Russ reached out for each other, trying to grab hands, but kept missing by inches.

Finally, after a superhuman lunge, Amy managed to grab Russ's sleeve, and they slowly pulled the two boats together.

While Nick and Russ held the two crafts together, Amy passed a waterlogged Ron onto the grassblade. The bottle cap was sinking fast.

"Come on, Amy!" Russ said, his hands out.

Before she could leap to the grass canoe, the cap abruptly sank, taking Amy down with it.

"Head for shore!" Russ yelled to the others, and dove overboard into the raging water.

He came up empty-handed. Holding his breath, he plunged beneath the waves a second time. A third. A fourth. Still no Amy.

* * *

His mother, quite pleased by her act of kindness, shut off the hose and left the yard.

"That looks *much* better," she said.

Riding their grass-blade boat, Nick and Ron crashed into a small mound of dirt. They climbed off the boat and collapsed on the ground, panting and coughing.

Nick staggered to his feet, scanning the river. "Amy?" he said, almost crying. "Amy?"

Then Russ surfaced, carrying the inert form of Amy in his arms. Gently, he placed her on the ground. Nick and Ron ran over.

Nick sank down. "Oh, *Amy*."

Ron pushed past him and an exhausted Russ.

"Outta the way," Ron said. "Scouts to the rescue."

He turned Amy onto her back and frantically — almost comically — began working her arms and legs as if she were some kind of pump. Amy didn't respond to his inept lifesaving skills, and Russ pushed him out of the way.

Nick and Ron watched nervously as Russ bent down over her and began to give her mouth-to-mouth resuscitation — Amy didn't respond. Russ dragged in a deep breath and tried again. And again.

By now, Nick was crying. "Wake up, Amy. Please?"

After what seemed like hours — but might have been minutes — Amy began coughing up water. She opened her eyes, coming face to face with Russ. They were both more than a little embarrassed. Behind them, Nick was sobbing with relief, and Ron was sniffling.

"What?" he said as Nick grinned at him. "I caught a cold, okay?"

Russ and Amy looked at each other, their faces still only a couple of inches apart.

"The question is," Amy said weakly, "is this heaven, or hell?"

Russ's laugh was just as weak. "You got me." He moved away from her and sat down, almost too exhausted to move. "You okay?"

Amy nodded, struggling to sit up. "I'm fine." She gave him a shy smile. "Thank you."

"My hero," Ron said, in an extra-high voice.

Nick punched him in the arm. "Don't be a jerk."

The tension broken, Russ and Amy helped each other up, leaning on each other for support.

Nick ran over, giving Amy a fierce hug. "I thought you were — "

"I thought *both* of you were . . ." Amy looked from her brother to Russ, gratefully.

"Hey, buddy," Ron said to Russ. "We missed you. We thought some Queen Bee *married* you, or something."

Nick, laughing, hugged Russ, too. "Nah," he said, "but you should have been on that bee — it was great! And then Russ made the bee crash, and it came after us, and we — "

Russ patted him on the head. "We can talk later. Now, we've got to head home."

"Aw, come on, Russ," Ron said. "We're tired."

"Listen to Russell," Amy said briskly. "We're

all together again. We have to be strong. We have to get home. We can't *dally* here."

"Dally?" Ron looked around. "Maybe he *should've* married the Queen Bee."

"I bet it's almost lunchtime," Ron said, and rubbed his stomach. "I bet Mom made hamburgers." He turned to Nick. "Saturday is hamburger day."

Both boys sighed hungrily.

"Let's go," Russ said.

Amy nodded. "Come on, troops."

They began their trek again. Ron, forcing himself to act like a scout, started singing "The Green Grass Grew All Around" as they marched. Nick joined in.

Russ and Amy smiled at them.

"Kids," Russ said.

"Yeah," Amy said.

The two boys, marching ahead of them, came to a stop, looking up at a wondrous object in front of them. There, illuminated by an almost religiously inspired shaft of sunlight, was a gargantuan Oreo cookie. Soggy from the "rainstorm," the cookie glistened magically like a cream-filled rainbow.

Ron was profoundly moved. "I think I've died and gone to heaven. It's like — the *American Dream*."

"It's as big as a house," Nick said reverently.

Ron nodded. "I'm hungry enough to eat it myself."

"Double filling," Nick said. "It has *double* filling."

The two boys ran forward to the cookie and

began grabbing handfuls of white cream filling and stuffing it into their mouths.

"I love this," Ron said, his mouth full. "I was *born* for this."

Nick stopped chewing when he saw a horrible sight. "Uh, guys?"

Over the top of the cookie appeared an army of antennae, twitching threateningly.

Ron backed away. "What is it?" He stopped next to Russ and Amy, seeing another group of antennae approaching from the rear. They were trapped. Surrounded.

"It's — *ants*," Amy said, too stunned to move.

Nick swallowed, white cream all over his face. "And they're *bigger* than us."

Chapter 11

For a few seconds, neither the four of them, nor the ants, moved.

Russ lifted up a leaf. "Under here — quick!"

They all dove underneath the cover of the leaf as the two hordes of ants descended upon the cookie. The ants swarmed over the massive Oreo, dismantling it with ease. Huddling under the leaf, Russ and the others talked in whispers as the insects milled around them.

"What *pigs!*" Ron whispered.

Nick began to sneeze, Ron glaring at him. Nick stopped.

"I — " — he tried to hold it back — "I'm allergic to — "

"*Now* is a bad time to be allergic," Ron said.

Once the cookie was dismantled, the ants began carrying large wads of it away.

"That's not fair," Ron protested. "That was *our* cookie." He stood up, fists tight. "I say we take them on!"

Russ yanked him down by the belt. "Don't move. They might think we're food."

"No way," Ron said. "Ants don't eat people."

"They don't eat *normal-sized* people," Nick said. "They might think we're crumbs, or enemy insects or something."

"Right," Ron scoffed. "They're only bugs — I squash them all the time."

"I wouldn't advertise that," Amy said, crouching lower as one of the ants' antennae twitched near her.

"Besides," Nick said, "ants can lift over twenty times their weight. That's like *us* lifting a tractor."

Ron shook his head. "No way."

"No, Ron," Russ disagreed. "That kind of sounds familiar." He looked at Nick. "How do you know stuff like that?"

"I don't know," Nick said, embarrassed. "I read a lot of books."

Russ nodded. "I guess *so*."

"Shhh!" Amy hissed, pointing beyond the leaf.

An ant walked over, looking curiously at the leaf. Seeing that Nick was about to sneeze, Ron reached over and grabbed his mouth, covering it. The ant tried to lift the leaf, while they tried to hold it down. The ant tried again, then lost interest, returning to what was left of the cookie.

Ron peeked out. "Whew. That was close."

The army of ants continued to carry off the leftover crumbs. Leaving last, carrying a huge piece, was a baby ant. It struggled with the huge wad of chocolate. Dropped it. Picked it up. Tried pushing it. Tried *pulling* it.

Ron grinned. "I think it's snack time."

"Get serious," Russ said.

"I have a plan." Ron tore off a stiff piece of grass and fashioned it into a spear.

Then, he charged the ant, yelling like a banshee, swinging his "spear." The little ant, panicking, dropped the crumb and began to run after the retreating colony.

"Don't let it get away!" Amy said, running after it. "It'll bring back the others!"

"Nice plan," Russ said to Ron.

Ron shrugged. "Time for plan number two." He sprinted after the ant and dove onto its back, cowboy-style. "Scouts to the rescue!"

The others caught up to him, laughing at the sight of Ron clinging to the ant's back.

"Ride 'em, cowboy!" Nick said, and jumped onto the back of the ant as well. The ant careened in scared circles.

"Okay, enough fun," Russ said. "Pull him over."

Up on the ant, Ron and Nick looked at each other.

"You heard Russ," Nick said. "Pull him over."

"*You* pull him over," Ron said.

Each of the boys grabbed an antenna and tried to steer the ant in one direction or another. It didn't work.

"We *can't* pull him over," Nick said, starting to get scared.

Amy shook her head in disgust. "Boys."

Russ charged the ant and tried to grab hold of it. The ant easily outmanuevered him. He dove and missed, slamming into the mud. Russ grabbed the ant by the neck and was carried along, heels dragging on the ground. He was thrown off, falling at Amy's feet.

"Pathetic," Amy said.

"Help!" Ron yelled. "I'm getting seasick!"

Russ glanced around, looking for some way to help. He grabbed Ron's grass spear.

Amy looked at the limp grass spear, then at the rampaging ant. Then she ran over to the fallen crumb of Oreo. She broke off a wad of chocolate and then walked directly in front of the charging ant.

"No, Amy!" Nick yelled, still clinging to the ant. "Look out!"

Amy stood her ground, and the ant skidded to a stop, Ron and Nick falling off.

"Gotta replace those shock absorbers," Ron said dizzily.

The ant slowly approached Amy, antennae pricked forward. Amy gazed into the ugly insect face, unable to keep from crinkling her nose up in revulsion. The ant didn't seem to notice, gently removing the small crumb from her hand and munching away.

While the ant was chewing, Russ moved up behind it and slipped a hastily fashioned grass lariat around its neck. The ant didn't even flinch.

Dizzy from their ride, the younger boys staggered up to Amy.

Ron put his hand out. "All *right*, Stretch. Stretch the Lion Tamer."

Amy smiled and shook his hand. They all stood there, watching the ant eat.

"Wow," Ron said. "A *bug pig*."

Russ looked around. "We can't just leave him here. He might bring back the whole colony."

"You know," Amy said thoughtfully, "if he'd let us, we could use him for transportation."

Russ looked dubious. "What?"

"I don't know," Amy said. "I mean, he moves a lot faster than we do. We could get through the yard in half the time."

They all looked at the ant, visually measuring his size.

"Ride him *again?*" Ron said, without enthusiam.

"Swell," Nick said, with even less enthusiam. "Can't wait."

"I don't know." Amy studied the ant. "He's too small to hold all of us."

"And it's not like we could *steer* him, anyway," Ron said.

They all looked at the ant, then Nick began to smile.

"I think I have an idea," he said.

Chapter 12

It took a while, but they managed to fashion an Indian-style sled with woven bits of grass and flower stems. Amy, Russ, and Nick sat on the sled, while Ron rode on the ant's back, wearing a flower leaf around his head like a turban and holding a stick with an Oreo crumb affixed to its end. He dangled the stick in front of the ant's head.

They rode through the grass forest, singing "And the Green Grass Grew All Around," while munching smaller crumbs of leftover cookie.

"Okay," Amy said. "Hang a left."

Ron tilted the stick to the left side of the ant's head. The ant veered left.

Ron smiled. "Who says junk food isn't good for you?" He looked back at Amy. "Where to now, Bwana-ette?"

Amy laughed. "*Home*, James."

Ron nodded, facing forward. "Tarzan's the name. Jungles're my game." He held the stick out in front of the ant's head, and the ant plowed forward.

Amy glanced at Nick, who didn't seem to be enjoying the sleigh ride at all. "Why so glum, chum?" she asked, trying to cheer him up.

"I wish Dad had thrown us out closer to the house," he said.

"It could have been worse," Ron called back.

"How?" Nick asked.

"*My* father would have thrown us down the garbage disposal," Ron said cheerfully.

Amy shuddered. "Ronald!"

Ron shrugged. "Well, he *would* have."

"Just shut up and drive," Russ said.

It was dusk, and a police car sat in front of the two houses. An officer stood at the Thompsons' front door, interviewing them.

"Any reason your kids would want to run away?" he asked, taking notes.

"No," Mrs. Thompson said. "None at all. Ron was in the yard, playing, and our older boy, Russ, was — " She stopped. "Oh, no. You don't think because he was cut from the football team — "

Mr. Thompson motioned for her to be quiet. "There's no reason my kids would run away. They're happy kids. No problems."

"Uh-huh," the cop said.

Mr. Thompson bristled at that. "What's 'uh-huh' supposed to mean?"

"Russell," his wife said in a warning voice.

Mr. Thompson frowned at her, too. "Well, I don't like the way he said 'Uh-huh.' It didn't sound *sincere*."

The police officer looked tired. "Did you have an argument with your son this morning, Mr. Thompson?"

"I don't argue with my kids, mister," Mr. Thompson said huffily. "I *discuss* things with them."

"Uh-huh," the cop said. "Did you discuss his getting cut from the team?"

Mr. Thompson scowled at him. "Now just what are you getting at?"

The cop didn't even blink. "Maybe he felt you were angry with him."

"*Me?*" Mr. Thompson said, furious. "Angry with him? I love those kids! I'm their father. I worship the ground they walk on." He kicked his foot forward, hitting a ceramic lawn jockey, sending its head rolling across the yard.

The cop looked at him impassively. "Uh-huh."

Mr. Thompson turned to his wife. "He's doing it again, Mae! Make him stop doing that!"

Next door, the Szalinskis were showing the police officer who has just interviewed *them* to the front door.

"Okay, folks," the cop said, sounding reassuring. "We'll tell all our patrol cars to be on the lookout for two kids and a couch. We'll check in tomorrow."

They watched him cross the yard to his car, then Professor Szalinski turned to go inside.

"You coming?" he asked, rubbing a tired hand across his eyes.

Mrs. Szalinski glanced over to the Thompsons'

house, where another police officer was leaving. "In a minute, dear."

As her husband went inside, she walked over to the Thompsons' front porch, where Mrs. Thompson was watching the police car pull away. They smiled sadly at each other.

"Hi, Diane," Mrs. Thompson said.

Mrs. Szalinski sat down on the front steps. "Hello, Mae. Kids still gone?"

Mrs. Thompson nodded. "I think they've run away."

Mrs. Szalinski tilted her head inquisitively.

"I *knew* Russ was upset this morning," Mrs. Thompson said, "but to run away? I keep telling Russell, go easy with the children. Don't get so excited." She let out her breath. "But he's just as much a child as the kids are."

Mrs. Szalinski nodded unhappily. "Wayne, too."

"Well." Mrs. Thompson stood up. "For better or worse, right?"

Mrs. Szalinski didn't answer right away. "Right," she said finally. When she walked into her house, her husband was tethering Quark to a long leash in the kitchen. Seeing her, Quark barked wildly. "Not *now*, Quark," she said. "Wayne, did you know that the Thompson children are still gone, too?"

"No," Professor Szalinski said, knotting the leash. "I can't figure out why Amy and Nick would have taken the furniture. Maybe they were upset about breaking the window."

His wife straightened up. "What window?"

He gestured vaguely above them. "In the attic. They threw a baseball through the window and hit my machine and — "

"Amy and Nick don't *play* baseball," she said. Their eyes met.

"The Thompson kids do," he said slowly.

"And *they're missing, too*," they said at the same time.

Professor Szalinski snapped into action. "I want to check something out. Come on." He headed for the attic, taking the stairs two at a time.

Once they were up there, he picked up the ball, tossing it to her.

Idly, she rubbed what looked like a burn mark on it. "It must belong to Ron."

He bent down to inspect the machine. "The override circuitry is damaged. I wonder if — no, surely . . . no."

"What?" his wife asked.

He got down on his knees, peering at the machine. "The ball is burned. It's possible that it activated the particle beams."

"What are you talking about?" she asked, very uneasy.

He didn't answer, crawling around the floor, setting down his arms and legs in an exaggeratedly careful way.

"Nothing," he said. "I just hope — *don't move!* Oh, *no*." Gingerly, he picked up a tiny piece of debris. He held it in the palm of his hand. He looked at the machine. Then he put it all together. "It works!" he said, elated. Then, he realized what *that* meant. "Oh, no," he said. "It *works*."

Chapter 13

"*What* works?" Mrs. Szalinski asked, trying to see what he had in his hand.

"Watch it!" he warned. "Watch where you step!"

"But — "

"Don't move," he said. "I'll come to you." One small, tiptoe step at a time, he walked over to her.

"So what *is* it?" she asked.

He held out a tiny, perfectly intact, beige couch — now smaller than a button. "My thinking couch," he said somberly.

She stared at him, dumbfounded. "You mean, you think the kids — ?"

"If the couch was affected, and the kids were up here, all of them — " He stopped, and they both got down on their hands and knees.

"Kids?" Mrs. Szalinski started crawling around the room. "Are you here?"

"Kids? Careful, now," he warned her. "Watch your knees."

"I know, I know." She crawled still more carefully. "Amy? Nick?"

After a few minutes of crawling, Professor Szalinski noticed the dustpan leaning against the wall. He jumped up; his wife gasped and covered her eyes.

"Get the flashlight! I'll get a magnifying glass!" He ran out of the room.

Cautiously, Mrs. Szalinski got up, then ran after him with long, light steps, wincing every time her feet hit the floor.

"What's going on?" she asked, following her husband. "Where are the children?"

"I swept out the room this afternoon and put the trash out in the yard!" Professor Szalinski pawed through his top dresser drawer, searching for his magnifying glass without success. He ran into Nick's room and found one on top of the desk. Mrs. Szalinski dug through the front hall closet, looking for a flashlight.

"Bring some tweezers, too!" he yelled, running out to the backyard.

She nodded, dashing upstairs to the medicine cabinet.

Outside, they worked together — slowly, delicately — going through the trash. Mr. Thompson came out and leaned against the fence. He took a cigarette out from underneath his hat and lit up, inhaling deeply. Then he stared, seeing his neighbors whispering into their trash bags and pawing through them. He leaned forward, trying — but unable — to hear what they were saying.

"Amy?" Professor Szalinski tweezed out a piece of runny egg. "Nick?"

Mrs. Szalinski pulled out a discarded piece of paper towel. "Can you hear us, kids?"

Professor Szalinski shined the flashlight, spotting a hole in the side of the bag. "Look," he said eagerly. "The kids must have made it from the inside, see?" He flashed the light on the ground.

His wife bent down in the grass. "You mean, you think they got out?"

He nodded. "They must have made it into the grass, and — " His eyes widened.

"What?" she asked. "What's wrong, Wayne?"

"The Pervis boy mowed the lawn today," he said.

They looked at each other in horror.

Professor Szalinski was the first to recover. "Over there." He pointed to several Hefty bags in the corner of the yard. "He raked up the grass."

They ran over and began opening the bags, sifting through the grass cuttings.

Standing at his fence, still unable to hear what his neighbors were saying, Mr. Thompson shook his head, taking a deep puff of his cigarette.

"Eggheads," he said. "They're the first to crack under pressure."

The ant continued to slog along, pulling the sled across the muddy yard. His pace grew slower and slower.

Ron turned to look at the others. "I think the antmobile needs to recharge his batteries."

"Okay," Russ said. "Let's take a break."

Ron slid off the ant, while the others climbed out of the sled. Russ tethered the ant to a sturdy stalk of grass.

"I'm tired," Nick said.

"We'll *never* get back," Ron said.

Amy put her arm around him. "Don't worry. Our father'll know something is wrong if we're not back by supper. He'll look for us."

Russ sat down heavily. "I don't think he'll *see* us."

Ron sat down, too. "He doesn't even know we're *shrunk*."

Nick joined the other two boys on the ground. Amy was the only one who wasn't giving up.

"He'll find us," she said stubbornly. "I know he will."

Russ elbowed Ron. "She's pretty gutsy."

"For a girl," Ron conceded.

Although they didn't know it, they were sitting quite close to the fence. Above them, Mr. Thompson was still smoking, watching the Szalinskis forage through the trash. Casually, he flicked the ashes off his cigarette.

On the ground, Russ was the first to hear the hissing sound.

"Look out!" he said, as flakes of molten ash the size of automobile tires began drifting down around them, sizzling into the soggy ground.

"Take cover!" Amy said, and they all ran.

The ashes continued to rain down, a large one landing on the leaf under which Ron was cowering, burning a hole right through it. Ron ran. He skidded into a small pond of horrible goo, sinking up to his waist. He tried to pull free from the puddle, which was covered with the bodies of large, dead flies.

"Help!" he yelled. "Quicksand!"

He struggled helplessly in the mire as the others darted out from their various shelters, running to the edge of the pond, ashes still falling around them.

"That *can't* be quicksand," Nick said doubtfully.

Ron lifted his hand with an effort, tasting the goop, then groaning: "Help! Syrup!"

Russ groaned, too.

"Syrup?" Amy looked confused. "How did *syrup* get in our yard?"

"Never mind, never mind," Ron squirmed around, digging himself in even deeper.

"Don't move," Amy said. "The more you move, the faster you'll sink."

Russ stuck his arm out toward his brother, but couldn't reach far enough and almost toppled into the pond himself. He managed to pull himself back. Ashes were landing around them.

"We'll make a rope," Amy said. "We'll pull you out. Keep calm."

Ron lay in the syrup, slowly sinking. His teeth were chattering and he was beginning to cry in breathless little gasps.

"Hurry," he whispered. "Please hurry." He turned his head to the left and saw the floating body of a half-dead fly. It was still buzzing a little. Terrified, Ron turned his head away to look at something else. *Anything* else.

Beyond the pond, Amy and the others were

tearing at grass fibers, tying them together. Russ yanked the knots to test them. Then they threw the rope toward Ron, falling far short.

Above them, Mr. Thompson took one last puff on his cigarette before tossing the butt away.

"More rope!" Amy said, as the grass rope fell short again. "We need more rope."

They grabbed at the grass around them, looking up as they heard a roaring, whooshing noise.

"What was *that?*" Russ asked.

They all ducked as the glowing, smoldering cigarette butt sliced through the air. It landed in the syrup, still burning, a tobacco meteorite.

The unlit section of the cigarette butt landed next to Ron — it was slowly burning in his direction. Realizing that he might be burned to death in a few minutes, he tried to struggle away from it but sank deeper into the syrup.

The others ran forward, trying to shield themselves from the heat.

"We have to push it away," Amy said, blocking her face with her hands.

"Here, give me a hand," Russ said, grabbing a tiny twig, which — to them — was the size of a log.

They dragged it over to the pond, extending it toward Ron, trying to prod the cigarette away from him. The twig was too short.

"Help!" Ron said. "It's going to burn me!"

"What do we do?" Nick looked around wildly. "I don't know what to do!"

Part of the cigarette ash fell off the butt with

a roar, landing in the syrup near them. They backed away, blocking their faces, as the ashes sizzled into the liquid. Ron watched, petrified, as some of the hot ash fell on the trapped fly, burning the insect as it sank beneath the surface of the goop.

Nick stared at the scene, backing away in apparent horror. He turned and ran full-tilt back into the forest.

"Help me!" Ron said, crying. "Please, help me!"

Chapter 14

"Think," Russ said to Amy. "We have to *think* of something."

"I'm trying," she said. "I just — I'm *trying*."

There was a crunching sound behind them and they turned to see the little ant charging forward, Nick on its back.

He held a cookie crumb suspended from a stick in front of the ant's face. "Come on, boy. Come on." He led the ant to the edge of the bog, then slid off him, tossing the cookie crumb to Ron. "Ron! Catch!"

Leaning forward, Ron managed to snag the soggy Oreo fragment. A glimmer of hope played across his face.

"I read you, baby-brain." He waved the crumb at the ant. "You! Here you go, boy. Come and get it."

The ant extended its antennae, honing in on the Oreo crumb. It climbed up a stalk of grass to the edge of the pond, and the grass slowly bowed down under its weight. The ant extended its antennae toward the crumb as the cigarette burned down lower and lower, closer and closer to Ron.

Then Ron dropped the crumb. All of them gasped as it disappeared beneath the goop. The ant twitched its antennae, unable to sense the crumb anymore.

"Go get another," Amy said, pushing Nick. "Quick!"

Nick shook his head. "That was the last of it."

Even though the crumb was gone, the ant stood firm on the grass blade and Ron reached up, grabbing hold of one of the antennae. Slowly, the ant backed down the grass, hoisting Ron up and out of the syrup to safety as the cigarette burned down to the syrup with a final fiery hiss.

Amy looked at Russ; Russ looked at Amy.

"Fortuitous," Amy said.

"Nick of time," Russ said. "If you'll excuse the pun."

They both grinned and went to join the others.

Nick stared admiringly at the ant. "He saved your life. Even when you dropped the crumb."

Ron gave the ant's head a fond pat. "He could've gotten wasted by the cigarette butt, same as me."

"You are one lucky pup, Ron," Russ said, patting the ant, too.

"Can we let him go home, Russ?" Ron asked.

Russ nodded.

Ron turned to the ant. "Okay, boy. You're free. Go find your family. Your parents are probably worried about you."

"Like ours," Nick said.

Amy approached the ant, extending a hesitant

hand, then gave it a gentle pat. "Good luck."

The ant marched off, turning once, twitching its antennae in what looked like a good-bye wave.

"I don't know if you can understand me or not," Ron said, "but from know on, I'm going to be good to bugs."

"Even mosquitoes?" Nick asked.

Ron thought about that. "*Except* mosquitoes."

The ant shambled off into the forest.

"Thanks for the help," Ron said to Nick. "You're all right, baby-brain."

"No problem, scout," Nick said.

The Szalinskis continued sifting through the bags of grass, finding nothing. Hearing a noise, Professor Szalinski trained the light on the garbage where the Thompsons' cat, Cicero, sat, a piece of discarded, egg-stained toast in his mouth.

Mrs. Szalinski gasped. "Do you think — ?"

"I don't know." He sighed. "I doubt it."

The cat grabbed another piece of eggy toast and ran off.

"We still have a bag left," Professor Szalinski said, without much energy.

His wife shook her head, tears in her eyes. "I-I can't."

"There's still hope," he said. "Come on, shine the light over here."

A very bright light flashed on them from behind, held by Mr. Thompson.

"Lose something, folks?" he asked.

They looked at each other guiltily, then Professor Szalinski stood up.

"If I, uh — " he coughed, "show you something — something really strange — will you promise not to get upset?"

"*Me?*" Mr. Thompson took a step back. "Get upset? Heck. I'm as cool, calm, and collected as they come."

"Come up to my lab," Professor Szalinski said.

Mr. Thompson took another step back. "Lab?"

"Uh, attic," the scientist said. "I meant attic."

Ron, covered with syrup, walked over to a puddle left over from his mother's watering.

"Help me wash this off, will you?" he asked, wading in.

Russ stepped into the puddle, splashing him, while Amy helped.

"I'm pooped," Ron said.

Russ nodded. "Me, too."

Russ looked up at the dark sky. "Maybe we should rest for the night."

"We have a lot of ground to cover tomorrow," Amy said, nodding. "I think."

Nick wandered away, then came to a halt. "Hey, look at this!"

The others sloshed over to join him, seeing several Stonehenge-sized monolithic structures.

Russ frowned. "What *are* they?"

"My Legos," Nick said.

The mammoth plastic blocks were square, with station-wagon-sized round indentations on the back.

Nick sat in one of the round indentations. "Pretty cosy."

Ron climbed into an adjoining round spot.

"Not bad," he said. "Better than our tent."

Russ stretched, still on the ground. "Try and get some sleep now, okay?"

"No problem," Ron said, his eyes already closed.

Russ and Amy walked over to another Lego, sitting on the square end. They gazed up into a picture-perfect, clear sky. There was a full moon lighting the area with a magical blue glow as fireflies twinkled in the air.

"Tired?" Russ asked.

Amy held back a yawn. "I'm okay."

"I'm so sleepy I ache," he said.

She nodded. "Me, too." She looked up at the sky. "Great moon."

"Yeah, it's — it's pretty full." Russ blinked, aware of how inane that had sounded.

"It's funny," Amy said. "The moon looks the same no matter *what* size you are."

Russ nodded, then gave her a self-conscious smile. "You want to hear something stupid?"

"Sure," Amy said. "I enjoy stupid things."

He grinned sheepishly. "No, I — "

"In fact," she said, "I *only* enjoy stupid things. Witless things."

"Finished?" he asked.

"Yeah. You can tell me the stupid thing."

"I just meant — " He shifted his position, ending up a little closer to her. "I mean, I've watched the way you handle Nick and the way you run the house, with your mother gone and all, and I just wanted to tell you that I think it's, uh, really — impressive."

Amy looked at him, surprised. "Thanks."

"Just, you know, wanted to tell you."

"I've watched you, too," she said, and flushed. "I mean, I've seen you working out and stuff. You're pretty good. I mean — I like watching you."

They didn't look at each other, embarrassed.

"Want to hear something *else* dumb?" Russ asked.

"Sure."

"Well," he focused up on the sky, "I've wanted to talk to you sometimes, but I've felt weird because — well, because you're, uh — "

"Taller?" she guessed.

"Yeah." He hunched his shoulders. "Dumb, huh?"

"Well, it doesn't make much difference *now*," she said. "What's the big deal if you're a quarter of an inch tall, or three-sixteenths?"

"Yeah."

They sat there for a minute; then Russ turned suddenly, kissing her.

"Does this mean we're friends?" she asked.

He laughed. "Yeah," he said, and kissed her again.

Chapter 15

Up in the attic, Mr. Thompson stood next to the Szalinskis, looking at the machine.

"Nice CB set," he said.

The professor flipped various knobs and switches. "Russ, the world of science is a mysterious, complex one — "

"Is this going to take long?" Mr. Thompson asked.

Professor Szalinski ignored that. "Each and every one of us is made up of countless, tiny particles moving around and — "

"Get to the point," Mr. Thompson said. "Get to the point."

" — and," Professor Szalinski went on, "what this machine does is analyze the molecular structure of — "

"Szalinski!"

He sighed. "I think this machine shrank our kids."

Mr. Thompson shook his head. "Say what?"

"This machine," Professor Szalinski said. "I think it shrank our kids."

Mr. Thompson laughed, looking at Mrs. Szalinski. Who wasn't laughing. He looked at Professor Szalinski. "What do you take me for — a complete idiot?"

"But, it's true," Mrs. Szalinski said, Mr. Thompson whirling on her. "I mean, about the machine."

"We have proof," Professor Szalinski said.

She placed the tiny thinking couch in Mr. Thompson's hand.

"So what?" Mr. Thompson said. "A toy? Big deal. That doesn't mean our kids have shrunk."

Professor Szalinski adjusted a few more knobs. "I'll show you. Put your cap on that pedestal."

Mr. Thompson held the hat protectively to his head. "My Giants cap?"

"Yes, yes," Professor Szalinski said impatiently. "You want proof, don't you?"

Mr. Thompson lifted the cap and a shower of cigarettes fell down. "I've had this cap for twenty years."

Professor Szalinski paid no attention, turning the machine on.

Gingerly, Mr. Thompson placed the cap on the pedestal in front of the metal wall.

"Okay. Step back and be amazed." The professor activated the machine, both beams skittering across the room.

"Big deal," Mr. Thompson said. "I have a lava light at home that works better."

"Watch when the beams connect," Professor Szalinski said confidently.

They all watched as the two beams connected

with the cap. The cap shimmered, then quivered, then exploded, sending bits and pieces of charred material everywhere.

Mrs. Szalinski was horrified; Professor Szalinski perplexed; Mr. Thompson furious.

"I don't understand it." Professor Szalinski looked at his machine. "It must have worked before."

"Are you saying my kids — that machine — *you blew up my kids?!*" Mr. Thompson made a move to strangle him but missed as the scientist bent down to examine the cap fragments.

"Of course not." Professor Szalinski studied a piece of the burnt material. "If they had blown up, we would have found — "

Mrs. Szalinski paled, covering her mouth with her hands.

"I mean, no," Professor Szalinski said. "They shrank. I'm positive."

"And *I'm* positive that you should be locked up." Mr. Thompson stepped up to Professor Szalinski, clenching his fists. "I don't know what your game is, Szalinski, but if I find out that you've done anything to my kids . . . I'll do to you what you did to my genuine number-one-in-a-series New York Giants Cap." He started to storm out of the room, glanced nervously at the floor, and tiptoed carefully out.

The inventor stared at the machine, unhappily baffled.

His wife came over, putting her arm around him. "How about a drink?"

He nodded and let her lead him downstairs.

They sat at the kitchen table, with half-empty

glasses of milk in front of them. He absentmind-edly fingered the magnifying glass, while she toyed with the flashlight.

"It's all my fault," he said finally.

"No. You're just — dedicated," she said. "I should have understood that. You have dreams."

"But I forget reality." He sighed, resting his head in his hands. "I ignore the people I care about the most."

"Oh, Wayne." His wife sagged down in her chair. "How could I have left you and the kids? If I had been here — if anything happens to them — " Tears began to roll down her cheeks.

He pulled his chair next to hers and put a protective arm around her. "We'll find them, hon. I promise. We'll find them."

She rested her head against his chest, crying. He swallowed hard, wiped a single tear from his eyes, and hugged her closer. On the floor, still tethered to his dog bed, Quark sighed.

Russ was the first to wake up the next morn-ing. He stretched and yawned, then looked around in the daylight to see where they were.

"I don't believe it," he said.

The sound of his voice woke Amy up. "What?"

He pointed and she saw that they were only yards away from the house, which was as tall as a glacier above them.

Amy gave him a big hug, then jumped up. "Nick! Ron! Come on, we're home!"

The two boys woke up, lazily.

"Huh?" Nick said, squinting in the bright light.

"Wuzzat?" Ron asked, his voice thick with sleep.

Then Nick spotted the house. "Hey, look!"

"All right!" Ron said, and he and Nick exchanged high fives.

Wide awake now, they chased after Russ and Amy, running to the end of the yard toward the back steps. There they slowed down, the excitement leaving their faces. They were standing in front of the biggest step in history. Not much of a step for mankind, but a *huge* step for them.

"It's, uh, a little bigger than I thought it would be." Russ looked around, picking up a small twig. He placed it against the step, where it looked pathetically small, like leaning a stepladder against a skyscraper. "Okay, okay, don't worry. I'll figure something out."

For the first time Amy's lower lip began to quiver.

Russ put his arm around her. "Don't worry, we'll make it. We just have to come up with a plan."

Tears began to dribble, silently, down her face, and the boys all looked at one another uneasily.

Nick approached his sister, reaching up to take her hand. "Amy? Don't cry. Okay, Amy? Come on. Even if the odds are against us — "

"The music should be swelling right now," Ron whispered to Russ.

Nick scowled at him and went on. " — so what? People beat the odds all the time, right?" He looked at Russ for help.

"Sure," Russ said, making his voice deep and

confident. "We've gotten this far."

"Yeah," Nick chimed in. "We've gotten through a flood."

"And killer bees," Ron said.

Russ nodded. "And a power mower."

"And maple syrup!" Ron said.

Amy sniffled and nodded, still crying. "But how are we going to get into the *house?*"

No one had an answer.

"Boy, though, that flood," Ron said. "That *flood* was something."

Nick stood up suddenly, smiling. Putting two fingers in his mouth, he let out a shrill whistle. He was winded after one try and wheezed, trying to catch his breath.

"What are you doing?" Russ asked, patting him on the back.

"Hitching a ride." Nick puffed out his chest again, forcing out a second, shrill blast.

Chapter 16

In the kitchen, Wayne and Diane were asleep at the table. Quark, still tied up, heard a very faint, very familiar whistle. His ears perked up, and he began to whine and pull at his leash. There was another whistle and he gnawed at his leash, trying to get away.

Outside, Nick's face was beet-red as he kept whistling.

"Quark will never hear you," Amy said.

Nick stopped, breathing hard. "Sure he will. Dogs have *great* ears."

Russ and Ron looked at each other, shrugged, and began to whistle and shout.

"Here, boy," Russ called.

"Yo, dog!" Ron shouted.

Amy looked at all of them and decided to join in. "Hey, Quark," she said, and let out a little whistle.

* * *

In the kitchen, Quark gnawed and gnawed, growling in frustration. He turned himself around and slowly pulled himself, backward, out of his dog collar, and ran for the swinging door leading outside. He pushed against it, but the door wouldn't budge. Hearing the shouts and whistles get more frantic, he pushed harder. The door wouldn't move.

Finally, he backed up all the way across the kitchen and hurled himself across the room. The door flew open and he rolled out and down the steps. Russ and the others scattered.

Quark picked himself up out of the dirt and stood there in confusion, hearing tiny little voices all around him.

"Good boy, Quark," Nick said proudly.

"Over here, Quark," Amy said, on his other side.

"Way to go, dog," Russ said, behind him.

Quark turned this way and that, trying to locate the voices' source. Finally, he zeroed in on one of them. On seeing the tiny people, people who had once been much bigger than he was, he whimpered.

"It's okay," Amy said. "It's us, Quark."

"We're just littler now," Nick said.

"Come on, Quark." Amy clapped her hands. "Lie down."

Quark sniffed at them and almost sucked them up his nostrils in the process.

Amy ducked out of the way. "Don't sniff, dumbbell. Lie down."

Quark did as he was told.

"Good dog," Amy said. "Now, stay. Stay, Quark."

"All aboard!" Nick said, imitating a train conductor.

Quark whimpered slightly as the barely larger-than-flea-sized people climbed up his ear and onto the back of his head.

"Nothing personal," Ron said, "but this dog needs a *bath*."

Nick sniffed, then sneezed. "Phew. He sure does."

"Everybody on?" Russ checked to make sure they were all there.

"Ready for takeoff," Ron said.

"Okay, Quark." Amy posted herself near his ear, hanging onto two tufts of reinlike fur. "Up the steps. Into the house."

Quark took the first step, then stopped short. Cicero was standing there, hissing, his fur puffed up. Quark growled.

"Oh, *great*," Russ said.

Amy tapped Quark's ear firmly. "Quark. Up the stairs, boy. *Don't* chase the cat."

While Quark hesitated, Cicero lunged after him. Panicked, Quark ran to the back of the yard, with Cicero in hot pursuit.

"Hang on!" Russ yelled. All of them grabbed tufts of fur to hold onto.

Quark scrambled over the trash bags and wiggled under the fence, Cicero right behind him. The dog started into the street and zigzagged in and out of traffic, yelping. Cicero skidded to a stop at the curb.

Russ and the others ducked as titanic cars and people passed by them. Horns blared. Tires screeched. People yelled.

"Whoa!" Nick shouted into Quark's ear. "Whoa, Quark!"

"Look out!" Amy shouted into his other ear, as two cars — one from each direction — bore down on them.

Quark stood in the middle of the road, paralyzed with fear as the cars sped toward him from both sides. Then, eyes shut, he cringed, flattening himself on the street.

There was a crash. Glass shattered, and deafening screeches and horns shook the sky.

Slowly, Quark got up. The two cars had crashed and were suspended, pyramid-style, above him. The two drivers, unhurt, were screaming at each other from inside their cars.

"Go *home*," Amy said into Quark's ear. "Go home *right now*."

Obediently, Quark trotted away from the accident, squeezing under the backyard fence and running up the back steps. Amy and the others were clutching at his fur to stay on.

"Go get Dad, Quark," Amy said as he ran into the kitchen. "Go to Dad."

The exhausted Szalinskis had fallen asleep at the kitchen table. Quark trotted over to Professor Szalinski's leg. He nuzzled the leg and pawed at it. Still asleep, Professor Szalinski swatted his leg with his hand. Quark leaped away, almost knocking his passengers off.

"We have to think of something better," Nick said, climbing up from where he had fallen onto

Quark's neck. "We'll get killed that way."

"Let's try yelling," Russ suggested.

"Mom! Dad!" Amy and Nick yelled together.

"Mr. Szalinski!" Russ shouted.

"Yo, Prof!" Ron screeched.

Professor and Mrs. Szalinski continued to sleep.

"Now what?" Russ asked Amy.

Amy shrugged. "You got me," she said.

Chapter 17

They all stood up on Quark's head, looking at Amy and Nick's parents.

"They'll never be able to see us from here," Russ said.

"Or *hear* us," Ron said, then paused. "They might see us if we were *on* the kitchen table."

"Good idea." Amy patted Quark's ear. "Quark. Up on the table, boy."

The dog cocked his head, not really believing her. Amy repeated herself. Quark stood up on his hind legs, flailing his front paws helplessly, much too short to manage it. As he stood there, they all started sliding off his head.

"Down, Quark!" Amy yelled, hanging on with one hand. The rest of her body dangled in the air. "Get down!"

The dog returned to all fours, his head straightening out. Then, just as they were getting their breaths, relaxing their holds on his fur, Quark spotted a chair. He scampered over to it and jumped up to the seat. Then he eased his nose onto the table, knocking over the sugar bowl in the process.

"Way to go," Ron said.

Russ grabbed his arm, pulling him up. "Just climb off him before he moves."

They ran down Quark's muzzle, jumping off onto the table. Then they ran over to Professor Szalinski, who was sleeping with his head on the table. They stopped by his ear and began yelling.

"Dad! Wake up!" Amy said.

"Come on." Ron pulled a strand of his hair. "We're right in front of your nose."

"*Ear*," Nick said.

"Whatever," Ron said.

"Professor!" Russ yelled at the top of his lungs.

No reaction.

"Dad's a heavy sleeper," Nick remarked to no one in particular.

"No kidding," Ron said.

Professor Szalinski continued to sleep, snoring loudly.

"We'll never wake them up," Ron said, sitting down on the place mat. "And when they *do* wake up, they'll need a neon sign to see us."

Nick looked at the mound of sugar Quark had spilled, then at Ron. "When explorers get lost in the snow, they make snow signs, right?"

"Yeah," Ron said, not getting it.

Nick pointed at the sugar.

"A sugar sign?" Ron asked.

Nick nodded.

Then Ron smiled, pointing to the abandoned magnifying glass. "That ought to help, too. Lion scouts to the rescue!" He charged over to the mound of sugar.

"It just might work," Russ said, and followed Nick and Ron to the mound of white crystals.

"We're going to need more sugar," Ron said, surveying the pile.

"No problem." Nick climbed inside the sugar dispenser and began tossing granules out. Ron caught them, tossing them to Russ and Amy, who began to fashion a sugar arrow, pointing toward the magnifying glass.

"When Dad wakes up, he'll *have* to see us," Nick said.

It took a long time to make the arrow, and just as they were finishing, they saw Professor Szalinski starting to wake up.

"All right!" Ron threw his hands up in a victory sign.

"Let's get to the magnifying glass," Russ said, herding them toward it.

Unfortunately, before they could move, Professor Szalinski launched into his habitual morning sneezes, causing a gale of wind across the tabletop.

"Hold on!" Amy yelled and they all clung to each other, buffeted by the wind as the sugar arrow blew away.

"Rats," Ron said.

"Just wave," Amy said. "Maybe he'll see us."

Her father stretched, sitting up as her mother opened her eyes, too.

"Oh." She winced, holding her back. "I'm stiff."

"Me, too." Professor Szalinski yawned widely.

"Want something to eat?" she asked.

"I guess." Seeing the overturned sugar dispenser, he reached down, setting it upright.

"Wait a minute," Amy said, looking around. "Where's Nick?"

They turned and looked at the sugar dispenser. Nick sat at the bottom.

"Oh, no," Russ said.

Nick banged on the side of the clear glass bowl, his voice muffled. "Get me out of here! Get Dad!"

"The magnifying glass," Amy said, moving quickly. "Let's get over there. Come on!"

"Hurry!" Nick's muffled voice yelled.

As they started to run, a large shadow fell over them.

"*Now* what?" Russ said.

Above them, Mrs. Szalinski set a bowl of Cheerios in front of her husband.

"The best I could do," she said.

He shrugged and poured milk on the cereal. Then he reached for the sugar spoon, sprinkled some on his cereal, and returned the spoon to the dispenser.

"Oh, no," Amy said. "You don't suppose — "

She and the others ran back to the sugar bowl, peering inside. Nick was gone. They turned to stare at her father as he picked up another spoon, bringing it down toward his bowl.

Inside the bowl, Nick was floundering around in the milk, perched in a Cheerio as if floating in an inner tube.

"Help," he gurgled. "Help! I'm allergic to

milk!" He looked up, seeing a flying-saucer-sized spoon heading for him. "Yipes!" He tried to paddle out of the way.

Oblivious, his father ate a spoonful of Cheerios.

Nick paddled furiously in the milk, gagging and choking.

His father moved his spoon back into the bowl, while Amy and the others screamed for him to stop.

"The magnifying glass," Russ said. "Hurry!"

Nick, Cheerio float and all, was lifted into the gigantic spoon.

Russ slid to a stop underneath the magnifying glass. "Everybody move around!"

"Shake it!" Ron said.

They jumped up and down, dancing and waving underneath the magnifying glass.

In the meantime, Professor Szalinski — unaware of Nick screaming from inside his Cheerio — lifted the spoon closer and closer to his mouth.

Chapter 18

Professor Szalinski, about to put the spoon in his mouth, looked down as Quark began barking and leaping around like a maniac. Professor Szalinski was about to yell at him when he glanced at the spoon in his hand for the first time. He gasped, seeing Nick waving frantically from the middle of a Cheerio.

"Oh, my!" He lowered the spoon, staring at it.

"Down there!" Nick squeaked, pointing. "Everyone else is down there!"

Professor Szalinski looked at the magnifying glass, his mouth gaping open.

"What?" Mrs. Szalinski followed his gaze. "What is it?"

"You're alive," Professor Szalinski said, close to tears. "You're safe!" Gently, he put the spoon next to the magnifying glass and Nick leaped out, running over to the others.

They all hugged, then waved up at the towering Szalinskis.

"Thank goodness they're all right," Mrs. Szalinski said, her voice shaking.

"You should have seen us ten minutes ago," Ron said, even though he knew they couldn't hear him.

She made a move to pick them up, and they all flattened as her husband restrained her hand.

"Don't touch them," he said.

She pulled her hand back. "Why?"

"They're too small to handle," he said. "We may hurt them."

She nodded, lifting her hands out of the way.

Gently, he lifted up the magnifying glass.

"Don't worry, guys," he said. "You're safe now. Wait right there."

They all looked at each other.

"Where does he expect us to go?" Ron asked.

Amy hugged Russ, who gave her a kiss.

"Everything's going to be all right now," he said, smiling. Professor Szalinski wiped the spoon clean on a dish towel, then brought it back to the table and set it down next to them.

"Can you make it up here?" he asked. His voice seemed to boom.

"No problem," Amy answered.

"I don't think he can hear you," Russ said, staring up at her father's huge, happy face.

"He doesn't have to," Amy said. "He can *see* me."

Nick was the first one to climb into the spoon. "Come on, slowpokes!"

The other three laughed and climbed in after him.

Carefully, Professor Szalinski lifted up the

spoon. Quark let out a big sigh of relief.

"Get the Thompsons over here," Professor Szalinski said, heading for the stairs. "I'll warm up the machine."

Quark followed him, wagging his tail happily.

"You're a hero, Quark," Amy said from the spoon. "That was a *two* Milkbone move."

Quark wagged his tail.

Up in the attic, once Mrs. Szalinski and the Thompsons had joined them, Professor Szalinski set the spoon in the target area of the room while his wife clutched Quark nervously in her arms. Mrs. Thompson stood next to her, biting her lip. Mr. Thompson was on her other side, dumbfounded, and — as usual — irate.

"You're a maniac, Szalinski," he said. "Do you realize what you've done? They're ruined for life!"

The professor crouched down in front of the machine, adjusting the computer, focusing on the spoon. "Don't worry, I have the atomic makeup computed."

"If you hurt them any more, Szalinski," Mr. Thompson threatened him with a fist, "I'll *personally* redo your house with my bulldozer!"

Professor Szalinski ignored him, trying to concentrate. "Now, I just have to figure the amount of space needed to be placed between their atoms."

"Please *hurry*," Mrs. Thompson said, wringing her hands together.

"It's done." He straightened up. "Now, to add an extra dollop of energy, to replace the energy they lost when shrinking — " He twirled a knob on the machine, then moved his hand to the "On" button.

Mr. Thompson tensed. "If you blow them up . . ."

Professor Szalinski hesitated, then withdrew his hand.

"What?" asked his wife, alarmed.

"He has a point." He rubbed his jaw with his hand, thinking. "I *haven't* gotten the machine to work properly. Only the kids have."

Sitting in the spoon, Amy and the three boys sighed.

"*Some* genius," Ron said grumpily.

"Give him time," Nick said. "He'll figure something out."

The nervous scientist paced up and down, scratching his head. "Somehow, the kids stumbled on something that I've been overlooking. Something — " He spotted Ron's baseball, still resting on the floor, and smiled. "Big Russ, toss me the ball, will you?"

"I oughtta *bean* you with the ball." He picked it up, throwing it only a little harder than necessary.

Professor Szalinski caught it, gazed at the burn mark on its side, and made some adjustments on the machine. "The answer has been right under my nose all the time!"

"You like baseball," his neighbor guessed.

"He *hates* baseball," Nick whispered to Ron.

"No, no, I've figured it out." Professor Szalinski stood up. "The machine uses two beams, a laser-tracking beam and the actual *shrinking* beam. The tracking beam focuses the second beam on the target. The reason things have been blowing up instead of shrinking is that when the beams collide, they generate too much heat. Yesterday, this ball must have blocked the tracking beam, and the shrinking beam worked all on its own. Now, all I have to do is shut off the one beam — " He threw the switch into the "On" position. The machine came to life with a hum, the beams jumping into space. "*Now*, all I need is a target."

"You *already* blew up my hat," Mr. Thompson grumbled.

The professor looked around, remembered the baseball, and tossed it in front of the beams. The ball was instantly zapped and miniaturized, falling down next to the spoon.

"*Told* you he'd figure it out," Nick said.

Mr. Thompson was very impressed. "Did you see that?" he asked his wife. "The egghead's no fool."

"Now," Professor Szalinski said, fiddling with the machine, "all I have to do is reverse the polarity of the beam and" — he turned a knob — "add some energy."

The machine hummed louder, the attic lights dimming and flickering.

"Come on," Professor Szalinski said. "You can do it. Come on."

The particle beams bounced out into the air as he tried to aim them.

"This *better* work," Ron said, sounding remarkably like his father.

"It will," Nick said. "It will."

The machine began to whine. One of the beams struck Russ, Jr., who began to grow and grow and grow.

Mr. Thompson's mouth dropped open, his gum fell out, and Quark's ears pricked straight up as Russ grew five feet tall. Six feet tall. Ten feet tall. Fifteen feet.

Then, his head cracked through the roof of the attic. His feet, supporting the too-heavy weight of his body — broke through the floor.

"Do something!" His mother screamed.

"I'm *trying*," Professor Szalinski said, twisting buttons and knobs. "I'm trying."

Chapter 19

"You idiot, Szalinski!" Mr. Thompson said angrily. "*Now* look what you've done!"

Professor Szalinski tinkered with his machine. "A few small adjustments. Not to worry."

Russ, now huge, reached down and picked up his father, holding him high in the air.

"Am I big enough for you now, Dad?" he asked.

"Russell!" Mr. Thompson squirmed in his hand. "I never — I mean — you were *always* big enough for me. You — put me down. *Please.* I'm sorry I yelled — I'll never yell at you again. You don't have to play football, you can play — *checkers* and it'll be fine with me. Honest!" He looked up at his son's large solemn face. "Please, put me down, son. Don't hurt me. I'm your *father*, Russell."

Russ smiled and put his father gently down on the floor.

"I'd never hurt you, Dad," he said. "I'm still the same old Russ. See, Dad, it's not how big you are on the outside — it's how big you are on the *inside* that really counts. Size doesn't mean anything."

Amy, Nick, and Ron clapped appreciatively.

Perspiring, Mr. Thompson wiped his forehead, then gave his wife a weak smile. "What a kid, huh?"

His wife smiled back, relieved. "Uh-huh."

As the professor adjusted the machine, Russ slowly shrank to his normal size.

"All right," Professor Szalinski spoke to the machine. "Just a little more power, just — " The machine began to smoke and sputter. Frantically, he read the computer printouts, trying to figure out what was going wrong. "Come on," he aimed the beams, "just a little more juice. A little more . . ."

There was a blinding flash of light and the room filled with smoke. Mrs. Szalinski, Russ, and the Thompsons flinched, backing away.

"Did it work?" Mrs. Szalinski asked. "I don't see — "

The other three stepped out of the remaining smoke. They were their normal heights again.

"All right!" Russ said, and gave Amy a big hug.

Their families joined them, and everyone hugged everyone else.

"I *knew* you could do it," Nick said, hugging his father. "You're something else."

Mrs. Szalinski hugged Professor Szalinski, too. "You *are* something else."

Professor Szalinski hugged the two of them and Amy all at once. "I promise you," he said,

"I'll never ignore you again. If you ever, *ever* think I'm doing that — "

"We'll make you eat Amy's eggs," Nick said, and giggled.

"Twerp," Amy said, but she laughed, too.

Russ and Ron stood next to their father.

Mr. Thompson and Russ turned to face each other.

"Son," his father started awkwardly. "If I've ever — well, made you feel bad about — well — " To his surprise, Russ gave him a big hug.

"Don't sweat the small stuff, Pop," he said.

Professor Szalinski unplugged the shrinking machine. "Hey, explorers," he said, terribly cheerful. "How about some breakfast?"

"Yeah!" the children yelled.

Mrs. Szalinski started for the stairs. "Pancakes and fresh maple syrup?"

Amy and the three boys all shuddered.

"No syrup," Russ said.

"*Please*, no syrup," Ron said.

The adults all exchanged glances, confused.

"It's a long story," Nick said.

The next Saturday Amy, Russ, and Nick stood up in front of a science conference. Nick was holding Quark.

"And then," Amy said, in the middle of her explanation, "my father used his amazing electromagnetic pulse device to restore our size."

Nick nodded. "It was *amazing*."

"Totally," Russ said.

115

Professor Szalinski smiled and stepped up to the podium.

"You asked for proof, gentlemen? Here's your proof." He indicated Russ and his children. "Three living subjects who have proven that size can be altered."

The scientists nearly laughed them out of the hall. Dr. Frederickson led the jeering.

"It's a fairy tale, Szalinski," Frederickson said. "You can hardly call the stories of — *children* — credible scientific proof."

The crowd continued to laugh, except for Dr. Brainard, who looked concerned. Professor Szalinski waited patiently for the hooting to die down, winking at his wife, who was also in the audience. She was sitting next to the Thompsons. Mr. Thompson was wearing a brand-new Giants cap.

"Stupid eggheads," Mr. Thompson said under his breath, frowning at the crowd of scientists.

"Anyway. I thought you might consider all of this farfetched." Professor Szalinski smiled and exchanged knowing glances with Amy, Nick, and Russ. "So I brought along a, um, visual aid. Dr. Frederickson? Would you be so kind as to open the back doors?"

Dr. Frederickson swaggered over to the doors, which burst open. Ron galloped into the room on the back of a now-giant ant. He held a full bag of Oreos in front of the ever-hungry insect, making the ant chase Frederickson around the room.

With a collective gasp, the scientists ran for cover.

"I love it." Mr. Thompson stayed in his chair, laughing his roaring laugh. "I love it!"

Dr. Frederickson was panting, terrified by the monster pursuing him. "Call it off!" he shrieked. "Call it off! You'll get the grant! Help!"

Leaning in a corner of the room, Dr. Brainard smiled, lighting his pipe. "Interesting," he said. "Very interesting."

Quark barked from the stage, then jumped out of Nick's arms and began chasing the ant chasing Dr. Frederickson, barking loudly.

Mrs. Szalinski and the Thompsons walked up to the podium. Mr. Thompson gave his neighbor a congratulatory slap on the back and the two men shared a hearty laugh.

Amy, Nick, and Russ stood on the stage, watching the scientists dodge and duck and scream.

"I think they're impressed," Nick said.

"Looks that way," Amy said, laughing.

Russ reached over to take her hand. "Sure does."

The Szalinskis were also holding hands, watching the scientists cower under chairs. Ron was whooping like Tarzan as he rode the galloping ant.

As the pandemonium went on, the Szalinskis and the Thompsons stood side by side, watching. Friends. Neighbors. The kind of just-plain-folks who live right down the street from you.

Well, almost.